THE RECLUSE OF LONGWOOD PRIORY

When Isabel's father is attacked and injured, father and daughter are given shelter by Edmund Carwell, the owner of Longwood Priory. Intrigued by the fleeting glimpses of their mysterious benefactor, Isabel seeks him out, only to stumble on his tragic secret. She succeeds in bringing laughter and music back to the Priory. But is her influence strong enough to heal old wounds and help Carwell come to terms with the legacy of his past?

JASMINA SVENNE

THE RECLUSE OF LONGWOOD PRIORY

Complete and Unabridged

LINFORD
Leicester

First published in 2005 in Great Britain

First Linford Edition
published 2005

British Library CIP Data

Svenne, Jasmina M.
 The recluse of Longwood Priory.—
 Large print ed.—
 Linford romance library
 1. Love stories
 2. Large type books
 I. Title
 823.9'2 [F]

ISBN 1–84617–108–3

Published by
F. A. Thorpe (Publishing)
Anstey, Leicestershire

Set by Words & Graphics Ltd.
Anstey, Leicestershire
Printed and bound in Great Britain by
T. J. International Ltd., Padstow, Cornwall

This book is printed on acid-free paper

1

'You'll never guess who it is,' Sarah Waite whispered excitedly. At the rap at the door, she had flown across the parlour to peer out of the window towards the doorstep of the parsonage. 'I expect he has only come to see Papa, but still . . . '

Isabel Locke could hear a man's voice in the hall, talking to the servant, and her heart jumped. Surely it couldn't be who she thought it was? She hadn't much time to prepare herself before the servant entered.

'Captain Davenant, ma'am.'

Sarah rushed forward to greet the guest, a tall, broad-shouldered man in the uniform of the Light Dragoons. Isabel rose in a daze. Christopher Davenant, or Kit as he was commonly known, was the squire's oldest son. Isabel had been in love with him since she was fifteen, despite the fact that he had never seemed to remember her name. But even so, during his long absence, she had forgotten how breathtakingly handsome he was.

'Miss Waite, how charming you look today,' he murmured, bowing low over Sarah's hand as she curtsied in reply. 'And Miss Locke too, what a fortunate dog I am.'

His grip on Isabel's hand was not as firm as she had expected and she was somewhat disconcerted. Perhaps he was being considerate because he did not want to hurt her.

'Papa is not at home at present if you wanted to talk to him,' Sarah said as they seated themselves, Captain Davenant making sure he sat between the two friends.

'So the maid told me. But I suspect that for my quest to be successful, I should beg you to become my allies.' He threw a warm look at Isabel to include her in his words.

'Of course, we'll help any way we

can,' Sarah asserted.

'While my regiment is billeted in town, my father would like to throw some entertainment in our honour. I thought perhaps a masquerade, they're all the rage in London.'

Sarah exclaimed and clapped her hands in undisguised delight.

'What do you want us to do?' Isabel asked quietly, afraid she was going to be overlooked.

The magnificent, soulful eyes turned towards her immediately. 'It's a very little thing. Public masquerades have such a bad reputation for licentiousness, I'm afraid some of the older people will forbid their sons and daughters from coming. I thought that if they knew such respectable gentlemen as the parson and the town's most esteemed attorney approved . . . ' He glanced at each of them in turn.

It was hardly likely that anyone would refuse, Isabel judged. Squire Davenant owned a manor house on the outskirts of the town, as well as a good deal of other property. Nothing he did could be judged amiss, surely.

'It will all be very innocent, I assure you,' he went on. 'Everyone there will be specially invited and no-one will be admitted without a ticket. If you could only persuade your fathers to let you come . . . '

'Oh, Papa can never refuse me anything,' Sarah replied airily, since Captain Davenant's eyes had come to rest on her at that moment. 'It is Mamma who will be harder to persuade.'

'And what about you, Miss Locke?'

Kit Davenant gazed at Isabel as if she were the most beautiful woman in the world and the masquerade would be a terrible disappointment without her.

'I don't think my father will object,' she said, though with a twinge of conscience at the thought of the expense. 'I'll do my best.'

'That is all I ask.' He included them both in a warm gaze. 'All the officers from my regiment will be there, so there will be no shortage of gentlemen to dance with.'

Sarah was voluble in the enthusiasm and Isabel was glad of it. It masked her own quieter pleasure. She had been to Davenant Hall a few times, but only at the larger, more public gatherings. The very thought of going to the ball, of mixing with the best sort of people, perhaps dancing with Kit Davenant was so overwhelming, she was afraid she would betray herself if she opened her mouth.

'I hope you will both grant me the pleasure of a dance.'

Isabel's voice caught in her throat. Not a single sound would come out.

'Only if you recognise us in our masks,' Sarah replied with a roguish grin.

They discussed the masquerade a good while longer before turning to other gossip.

'What's this I hear about the heir of Longwood Priory being a recluse?' Captain Davenant asked eventually. 'I thought that after the old man died, his grandson would be more lively company.'

Longwood Priory, a former monastery, had been the home of the same family since the Reformation. It was several miles away and ever since Isabel could remember, it had belonged to Old Mr Carwell, an invalid who still managed to outlive his only son. She had a vague memory of talk about Edmund Carwell, his grandson, coming to visit him, but if she had seen him as a child, she couldn't remember it.

'It's true, I'm afraid.' Sarah sighed. 'That house must have been cursed by the monks that were driven out of it. We had such high hopes when we heard Mr Edmund Carwell was unmarried, rich and young — well, at least, not old. I thought he would hold extravagant parties at Longwood. They say it's very beautiful, especially in moonlight. But he wouldn't even see Papa when he called and is probably horribly disagreeable.'

'Has no-one seen this Carwell since he arrived in Nottinghamshire?' Davenant persisted.

'No-one except his servants and he brought most of them with him from wherever he lived before, and they're all fiercely loyal and won't spread any gossip.'

Captain Davenant leaned back in his seat. 'It would almost be tempting to try to flush him out of his den. The shooting in that place must be magnificent, in the right season, with all that woodland.'

Isabel stayed much longer at the parsonage than she had intended. Kit Davenant by far outstayed the customary fifteen minutes for a courtesy visit and, with both of Sarah's parents out of the house, Isabel felt she ought to chaperone her younger friend. Or at least that was the excuse she would give if anyone questioned her about her long visit.

The officer was only driven away by the return of Mrs Waite. Isabel was a little disappointed he didn't offer to escort her home, but she assumed he must have other calls to pay. Anyway, this way she would be able to drift home, thinking about all he had said and anticipating what might happen at the masquerade. Perhaps hidden behind a mask, she would dare to say things she could never say to his face. If Papa would let her go.

'Isn't he handsome?'

Isabel echoed Sarah's sigh as they gazed after the mounted figure as it passed the window. Captain Davenant sat a horse well, showing off the shape of his leg and shining boot against the flank of his black stallion.

'Handsome is as handsome does,' Mrs Waite remarked, not unkindly.

'He's too far above either of us, I'm afraid,' Isabel said. She was a full four years older than Sarah, she reminded herself, and it was about time she stopped sighing for the moon.

'Well, stranger things have happened,' Sarah retorted, patting her curls into place. 'We're both respectable, even if you are a lawyer's daughter and I am only the parson's youngest child.'

'That reminds me, how is your father after his journey?' Mrs Waite intervened.

Mr Locke's presence had been necessary at the Spring Assizes in Nottingham and he had been supposed to return the previous evening. Isabel's face darkened.

'What's the matter?' Sarah asked, cocking her head. 'Didn't your father bring you home a nice present?'

'Papa didn't come home at all last night, though I sat up for him,' Isabel replied.

There was no point in telling Sarah there was no longer any money for extravagant presents. Her father, for all his astuteness in other people's business, had made an unfortunate investment some years previously and lost a good deal of money. The merchant ship in which he had had a share had been lost with all hands somewhere on the coast of Africa and with it had gone most of Isabel's marriage portion. Hence, at the age of twenty-five, she was teetering on the edge of spinsterhood.

'You don't think it is serious, do you?' Mrs Waite asked, suddenly grave. 'I'm sure it is only that business took longer than he expected and he decided to stay overnight.'

'Yes, I know. And sometimes he forgets to send me a note to say where he is. It's just that if anything happened to him, I would be all alone in the world.'

'You'll never be alone while there's a Waite left alive,' Sarah declared stoutly. 'You could come and live here with us. Papa and Mamma would insist on it, wouldn't you, Mamma?'

'Naturally,' Mrs Waite replied, half-exasperated, half-amused.

'Thank you.' Isabel squeezed Sarah's hand. She was a nice girl, and always had been, in spite of being spoilt rotten by both her parents, two older brothers and an older sister. Isabel would not have exchanged her father for the world, but she could not help sometimes wishing that at least one of her siblings had survived childhood.

She pulled out her little watch, a relic of more prosperous days.

'I'd better go,' she said. 'Papa may have returned, if he set out directly after breakfast. Please give my regards to Mr Waite.'

The parsonage, a square house of honey-coloured stone, stood near the edge of a small market town. It was still only mid-March, but it was warm and summery in the sun.

Home to Isabel was a modestly-sized house in a street mainly consisting of prosperous shops. The Lockes had been forced to move to smaller premises as part of their retrenchment when the ship was lost, but thankfully her father still had plenty of clients. They only employed one maid at present, but Papa had hopes that in another year they might be able to afford a manservant or a second maid.

Isabel's heart sank as she entered the house. There was no sign of her father's hat or his walking stick in the hall. She retreated to the parlour and took up a book, but she could not concentrate.

Someone had stepped on her hem coming out of church the previous Sunday and she ought to mend it before the end of the week. The beauty about plain sewing was that it left her mind free to wander. To prevent herself from brooding on her father's absence, she allowed herself to dream about Kit Davenant and the sensation she would cause somehow at the masquerade.

It was odd, now she thought of it, that such a handsome man was not yet married. Perhaps God had heard the prayers she made ten years ago and kept Kit single for her sake, so he would come home and find her grown up and beautiful.

Beautiful. Hmm. Isabel turned towards the mirror and stretched up on tip-toe to get a good look at herself. She was not, she had to admit, conventionally beautiful. Handsome was how kindly people put it. Her face was a little too broad; her eyes a little too small and not quite blue enough; her nose was straight, for which she was grateful, but there was no denying it was on the large side.

'You'd look ridiculous with a little snub nose like Sarah Waite's,' her mother had told her more than once, when she was still alive.

However, Isabel judged she did not look too bad today, especially if her face was viewed in profile rather than directly. Her blue gown, open at the front to reveal a matching petticoat, made her eyes look bluer and brought out golden lights in her ordinary brown hair.

With the aid of curlpapers and uncomfortable nights, it fell in ringlets around her shoulders and she had naturally pale skin, blighted only by the faint suggestion of freckles around her much-despised nose.

She delayed dinner until it became

clear her father wasn't going to return just yet and Eliza, the maid, muttered something about the food being spoilt. As time wore on, Isabel began to grow seriously concerned and Eliza's jerky movements as she went about her work suggested that she too was uneasy.

The clatter of passing carriages made her glance up at the window. Unfortunately the milliner's shop outside was extremely popular, so Isabel's hopes were often raised, only to be dashed. Once she heard a knock at the door, but it was only someone wanting to consult her father and Eliza explained that Mr Locke was not yet home.

The long day drew to a close. Unable to see what she was doing any more, Isabel rang for Eliza to fetch the candles and draw the curtains. She had not quite completed the latter task, however, when Isabel heard the rattle of another carriage as it drew to a halt outside the house.

The loud rap made both women start and Eliza scuttled off to answer the door. Isabel listened, but it was not her father's voice, nor any she recognised.

'There's a letter for you, Miss,' Eliza said, bobbing a curtsey as she entered. 'The man says he was told to wait for an answer.'

Finally there was news from her father, Isabel thought, though it struck her as odd that she was expected to send a reply. But as she took the letter, her heart sank in disappointment. It was not her father's hasty scrawl.

In fact, she did not recognise the handwriting at all. If it wasn't absurd, she would almost have guessed it was a man's hand, large, firm and beautifully legible. But no gentleman would write to an unattached female unless he was related to her or a very close friend. Just for a second, the possibility that it might be Captain Davenant flitted across her mind.

She broke the seal and unfolded the

sheet, her heart beating so fast, she felt as if it would choke her.

Longwood Priory, 15th March, 1771

Dear Miss Locke,

I hope you will forgive a stranger for addressing you, but I am afraid I have some distressing news to impart to you.

Your father was attacked and injured by footpads on his way home from Nottingham last night. Fortunately one of my servants found him not far from the gates of my house and naturally he has been brought here.

A doctor has been to tend his wounds and he assured me there is no danger to his life, but he is very weak and has been asking for you. You are welcome to stay here and nurse your father until he has recovered sufficiently to return home. My coachman has instructions to bring you here and an apartment has been prepared for you next to your father's room. I hope you will have no qualms about accepting my invitation.

Your humble and obedient servant,

Edmund Carwell.

2

It was only after they set out that it occurred to Isabel that she had no idea what would be waiting for her at her journey's end. It had all happened so quickly. One minute she had been re-reading the letter, the next her bag had been lifted on to the roof of an old-fashioned carriage and she had been helped inside.

At first all her fears centred on her father. Suppose the doctor had made a mistake, or the mysterious Mr Carwell had lied to spare her feelings? Suppose her father was dying? But as they went on, she couldn't help remembering all the speculation there had been about the new master of Longwood Priory. Suppose the letter was a fraud, a cruel hoax? Would a recluse really invite a complete stranger into his house?

They barely paused at the turnpike,

since the coachman had purchased a ticket for his return journey. They passed through a village, now almost entirely in darkness. Isabel knew they had not much farther to go. It was a bizarre situation. She was travelling alone in the dark to the house of a man she did not know to tend her injured, perhaps dying father.

They stopped and Isabel heard the clang of wrought-iron gates. Then the carriage resumed its jolting pace, following a long, twisting driveway between banks of shrubs and overhanging trees, whose branches interlaced above her in a dark tunnel.

Just when she thought the drive would go on forever, they emerged into pale moonlight. Wide lawns spread on either side and in front of her a massive edifice was silhouetted against the sky. Adjoining the main building, there was a high wall with an empty, arched window, through which the stars gleamed.

A single light twinkling in an upper

window was the only indication that the house was not an abandoned ruin. As Isabel climbed out, she glanced up in time to see the silhouette of a man pass in front of the window, then vanish.

She had no time for wondering. A door was thrown open at the opposite end of the façade and light flooded out, illuminating a staircase up to the first floor of the priory. As Isabel hesitated, a motherly-looking woman in a black gown and white cap and apron bustled down the stairs, her stays creaking with every movement.

'Miss Locke?'

'Yes!'

'Welcome to Longwood Priory. Poor child, you look quite wan. There, there, your father's in good hands. I'll take you straight up to see him.'

'Thank you, Mrs — ' Isabel stopped, unable to remember if the woman had given her name.

'Mrs Beecroft, Mr Carwell's house-keeper. I'm forgetting my manners.' She twinkled cheerfully at Isabel, who felt too stunned to do more than smile feebly in return.

She was even more stunned a moment later when Mrs Beecroft hurried her from the vestibule into a vast hall, twice the size of Squire Davenant's drawing-room. It was panelled in wood with long, many-paned windows looking out on to the drive.

'This is the shortest route,' Mrs Beecroft explained, crossing the seemingly endless space towards a door and three steps leading up into a narrow passage. Through smaller windows, Isabel caught sight of a courtyard round which the house was built. Instead of turning left towards the room with the lighted window, the housekeeper veered to the right. Isabel followed in silence.

They turned the corner twice to reach the opposite wing. Here a short flight of steps led up to a small suite of rooms. Mrs Beecroft opened the farther door. There was only a dim light burning in one corner, but even so Isabel caught her breath.

The furniture was old-fashioned, but so well-cared for, it gleamed. The canopied bed lay at the far end of the room. Its green and gold curtains matched the tapestries, which hung from the walls, and Isabel felt ashamed to step on the carpet with her dusty shoes. But this consideration flew out of the window when she caught sight of her father between the parted curtains.

'Papa, what have they done to you?'

She ran across the room to lean over him. Mr Locke was past fifty now, but Isabel had never realised that he had grown any older than he was when she was a little girl. For the first time, she noticed wrinkles in his face.

He wore a nightcap, but it was partially dislodged by a bandage wrapped round his head. One of his eyes was nearly shut by a vast blue-black bruise. His lip had been cut and his mouth was swollen, but worst of all he could only extend his left hand towards her, creeping like a spider across the covers, because his right arm was heavily bandaged.

'It looks worse than it really is,' her father assured her, his voice slurred due to his stiff lip. 'Apart from a broken arm and a few cracked ribs, all I have is cuts and bruises.'

Isabel could not suppress a shudder, as she perched on the edge of the bed. It was so high, her feet dangled a good twelve inches above the carpet.

'I'll leave you in peace,' Mrs Beecroft said from the door. 'Your room is next door, Miss Locke. If you need anything, just ring.'

Isabel remembered her manners just in time to thank Mrs Beecroft before she shut the door and creaked away.

'She's a very obliging woman,' Mr Locke remarked.

Isabel glanced at the bedside table. It held everything an invalid could possibly want, a bottle of laudanum to numb the pain, a book in elegantly tooled covers, a dish of what had once been hot, sweet tea, a half-empty glass of wine . . .

'Tell me what happened, Papa. Why

did you not send for me sooner?'

Her father turned his head away from her, as if he was trying to evade the question.

'I was coming home last night, when I heard a cry. It wasn't even dark yet, no more than twilight, and I didn't think it would delay me much.'

He smiled ruefully as he paused for breath. The damaged ribs obviously caused him some discomfort, but he didn't want to draw attention to it, so Isabel made no comment.

'The trees were quite dense so I didn't see the man immediately. He was lying by the ditch and a horse was grazing nearby, so I thought he must have fallen and needed help to get to the village.'

Isabel shivered again. She thought she could guess what happened next.

'It was an ambush, wasn't it?'

Her father nodded slightly. 'As soon as I had dismounted and stooped over the man, he leapt up and someone else attacked me from behind. I know I struggled with them for a while, trying to reach my pistols, and then something struck me on the head and I don't remember any more.'

'Did you get a good look at them? They mustn't be allowed to go unpunished.' Isabel felt herself boiling with indignation. How could anyone take advantage of a good deed like this? She guessed her father's arm had been broken as he tried to shield his head and face from repeated blows.

'It all happened so quickly. I doubt I'd recognise them if they were close to me as you are now. All the money I had on me is gone and Mrs Beecroft tells me none of the servants found my horse, so I suppose they took that too. I ought to be grateful they let me keep my watch.'

This was probably not an act of generosity. Isabel and her father knew better than most that watches were comparatively easy to identify, and therefore clever thieves left them behind.

'I was lucky I was found when I was, the doctor says. If I had laid there all night in the dew, I could have caught a fever.'

'But if they found you last night, why did you not send for me?'

This time he did not refuse to answer, but he squeezed her hand reassuringly.

'It's very simple, child. I was unconscious for several hours and confused when I did wake, and those scoundrels took all the papers in my pockets, so Mr Carwell's servants had no means of guessing who I was. The doctor says I should not be moved until the bones have knitted properly,' Mr Locke added, 'and Mr Carwell insists that we should both stay here till then.'

'You've seen him, then?' Isabel asked. 'Mr Carwell, I mean.'

'No, but Mrs Beecroft brings notes and messages from him.'

They talked for a while longer until Mr Locke insisted she should go to her room and rest. He looked worn out, so

Isabel kissed him cautiously, afraid of jarring his wounds, before she ventured into the adjoining room.

If anything, this room was more beautiful than the first, though smaller in size. Isabel circled it in awe, hardly daring to touch the polished surfaces of the furniture. Her portmanteau had been unpacked and her possessions looked very plain and lonely amid this grandeur.

She caught sight of herself in the full-length mirror and could not help thinking she looked like a little girl lost in an adult world. She ran her fingers down the shimmering curtains and the twisted posts of the bed and pressed the mattress to test its softness. She could hardly imagine sleeping in a bed large enough to be a small room.

A tap at the door made her start guiltily and she sprang away from the bed before she called, 'come in', so no-one would guess she had been touching it. A young maid with a starched apron and cap entered, carrying a steaming jug.

'Mrs Beecroft sent me, ma'am,' she said, bobbing a curtsey. 'She thought you'd like some warm water to wash in.'

'That's very thoughtful of her.'

Had Mrs Beecroft perhaps guessed that Isabel was too overawed to ring the bell for assistance? The maid had been clearly given instructions to wait on Miss Locke and Isabel accepted her help to get undressed and brush out her hair.

★ ★ ★

Isabel woke at dawn. Unable to sleep, she crept across to the window. Directly beneath her room, there was a formal garden in the French style, set out with gravel paths, box hedges and beds in geometric shapes.

A footstep attracted her attention. There, beneath her window, stood a man. There was not a scrap of braid on his coat and his tricorn hat was ornamented only with a single white

28

feather. But something about his bearing proclaimed that he was a gentleman.

His back was turned towards the house and she could see he had dark hair, tied at the nape of his neck with a length of black ribbon. She willed him to turn round so she could catch a glimpse of his face, but he strode away without looking back and vanished in the direction of a walled garden she could see in the distance.

The room was chilled, so she crept back into bed and accidentally fell asleep again, only to be awakened by the same maid bringing her a cup of hot chocolate to sip in bed. She helped Isabel dress so she could take breakfast with her father in the next room. Only the severity of the bruises on his face reminded Isabel that this was not a dream.

Mrs Beecroft stepped into the room after the breakfast tray had been removed.

'Everything to your satisfaction, sir?'

'I don't know how to thank you enough,' Mr Locke replied.

'Oh, I can't take any credit for this. I take my orders from my master.'

'Do you think he might be able to able to spare a moment?' Isabel asked. 'We would like to thank him ourselves.'

For the first time in her experience of her, Mrs Beecroft looked uncomfortable and would not meet her eye.

'I'll speak to him about it,' she said and hastily changed the subject. 'Mr Carwell thought you might prefer to take all your meals here together, the great hall is rather large and lonely.'

Nor would it have been proper for Isabel to dine alone with the master of the house, so she consented gratefully.

'My master also asked me to tell Miss Locke that she is free to explore the house and grounds whenever her father is resting,' the housekeeper went on. 'Perhaps if you've no objection, sir, I could show her around a little.'

And so Isabel found herself following Mrs Beecroft round the gallery and up and down odd flights of steps into various rooms.

'This is the library,' Mrs Beecroft announced, opening a door in the north gallery. 'Your father tells me you are fond of reading and music and Mr Carwell says you are welcome to borrow any books you like and play the harpsichord, though I'm afraid it needs retuning.'

It was a long room, with a door at either end. As well as bookshelves down one wall, there were comfortable chairs in small groups and a harpsichord at the far end of the room. Peeping through the window, Isabel saw a strip of lawn running alongside the house. On her left, towards the front of the house, she could see the single wall with its vast, empty window.

'It looks almost like a ruined cathedral,' Isabel remarked.

'That's all that remains of the church that was attached to the priory. The rest was pulled down in the time of Henry Eighth, or thereabouts,' Mrs Beecroft explained.

The south wing was dominated by the drawing-room. A dozen family portraits hung on the walls. There were gentlemen in ruffs or large cavalier hats and ladies in rigid farthingales or shimmering silks with slashed sleeves and Nell Gwyn ringlets clustering around their faces. There was a family resemblance between the portraits and Isabel wondered if the present master looked like them.

'There's room for just one more,' she remarked as she reached the far end of the room, but as she spoke, the sun came out from behind a cloud and illuminated the wall.

With a start, Isabel noticed a rectangular patch, slightly brighter in colour than the rest of the wallpaper. There had been a portrait there once and for some reason it had been removed.

'You can reach the gardens by going down the stairs at the front of the house,' Mrs Beecroft explained hastily, before she could ask any questions.

'And this staircase goes down to the cloisters.'

Isabel followed her down the stairs. It was dark, damp and dismal down there, with vaulted ceilings and strange carvings. It seemed as if very little had changed since the sixteenth century.

'These rooms aren't used much,' Mrs Beecroft explained, 'so on a bad day, you could walk around the cloisters for hours without disturbing anyone.'

Life did not grow any more real as time passed. The doctor called every day to make sure Mr Locke's injuries were healing properly. Squire Davenant came too in his capacity as a magistrate, to see what information Mr Locke could give about his attackers and his stolen property, with a view to offering a reward for the conviction of the guilty parties. But apart from that, Isabel saw nobody except Mrs Beecroft and the servants.

She was tentative about accepting favours at first. When she examined the shelves in the library, she found herself constantly glancing over her shoulder, as if someone was watching her. The harpsichord seemed so loud when she first touched a key, she sprang back instinctively as if she had been burnt. But she seemed to disturb nobody and so grew more daring.

The garden had been neglected in the lifetime of its previous owner and was rather wild and overblown, adding to its weird beauty. When Isabel tried walking in the formal garden, she could feel the windows of the house watching her like countless eyes.

There were a number of walled gardens, mainly kitchen gardens, but also one full of leafless rosebushes. To the south of the house, a river had been dammed to form a lake and the woodland began on the opposite shore.

As her father recovered, Isabel sometimes went for longer walks there, to listen to the birdsong and watch the spring flowers creep out of sheltered nooks. Occasionally she saw a gardener, digging, planting or trundling away dead vegetation in a wheelbarrow, but otherwise she had the place to herself.

That was what was so unnerving, she decided as the days passed and she still had not been introduced to Mr Carwell. She had tried asking Mrs Beecroft about him, but the house-keeper, communicative on all other subjects, would tell her nothing, except that her master had his reasons.

'If I did not know better,' Isabel wrote in a letter to Sarah Waite, 'I would almost think Mr Carwell did not exist, or that he was away from home.'

This was not the case, however. Baffled by the absence of their host, Mr Locke had dictated a letter to Isabel, thanking Mr Carwell for his hospitality, and received a reply in the handwriting Isabel recognised.

Occasionally from the opposite side of the courtyard, she would see the figure of a man gliding along the gallery and once, from the window of the great hall, she saw a mounted figure, heading in the direction of the woodland.

Nearly a week passed without any closer contact with the master of Longwood Priory. Then one evening as she returned from a walk at dusk, Isabel noticed a light burning in the same window as on her arrival. Intrigued, she ventured to the northwest corner of the gallery and discovered a spiral staircase leading upwards. She could hear a man's voice from above. It was too far away to make out any words, but she could tell it was an educated voice, low and resonating.

She heard Mrs Beecroft say something in reply, then a door opened and shut and steps came towards her. Afraid of being caught prying, Isabel whisked into the library. To her relief, she heard the housekeeper turn in the opposite direction.

She closed her eyes and suddenly remembered her first glimpse of Mr Carwell. Perhaps he always took a walk early in the morning. Perhaps that was how she could meet him.

She rose before dawn, because she

knew it would take time to dress without assistance and she did not want the servants to know what she was planning. As she glanced up from fastening the jacket of her riding habit, she caught a glimpse of a man emerging from round the corner of the house. He seemed to be making his way towards the rose garden. Maybe if she hurried, she could intercept him.

Closing the door softly behind her, Isabel pattered down the steps and along the gallery, forcing herself to walk at a respectable pace. All the while she was calculating in her head, trying to work out which route Mr Carwell had chosen.

Only when she reached the great hall did she begin to run. The outer door slipped out of her hand and she winced guiltily when it slammed shut behind her.

She was breathless and unable to run any more, hampered by her stays and her long petticoats. And she must not look dishevelled, if she did meet him.

Moderating her pace, she took the path by the lake, which led her to the ivy-grown walls of the kitchen garden.

There was no-one there. Frustrated, she paused for a moment. She could not be defeated so easily. She knew her way around pretty well by now. If Mr Carwell had come this way, he would have had to pass her. Perhaps he had come no further than the rose garden before doubling back on himself, in which case she was at a distinct disadvantage.

Nevertheless she went on, the gravel crunching beneath her half-boots. Her panting seemed too loud, like that of a trapped animal lying low during a pursuit. A robin landed on a spray of ivy, causing it to sway violently and making her jump.

Almost randomly, Isabel made her way to the formal garden beneath her window, where she had last seen him, but she knew in her heart of hearts it was hopeless. He was long gone.

There was one more thing she could

do, she decided, as she forlornly made her way back to the house. Instead of returning to her room directly, she went to the foot of the spiral staircase. Everything was silent above. Perhaps the master of the house had not returned yet. Perhaps she could wait here in the shadows.

Her hands were clammy and shaking. Was this really a good idea? Even while she hesitated, she was alarmed by heavy footsteps behind her. She whirled around to make a hasty retreat, but she was too late. A tall figure in a dark blue coat blocked off her escape along the west gallery.

Isabel's smile froze on her lips, as the man belatedly turned his head aside. The sun had caught his face, revealing what he had tried to conceal. Isabel had already seen the disfiguring mark that had ravaged the left side of his face.

3

'What the devil are you doing here at this hour?' His melodious voice sounded so harsh, Isabel felt it like the lash of a whip.

'I'm Isabel Locke,' she stammered, but he cut her short.

'I know perfectly well who you are. You waylaid me deliberately, didn't you?'

'I, I only wanted to thank you for — '

'Has one of the servants been gossiping? Did your curiosity overwhelm you? Did you want to see the freak?'

Before Isabel could stammer out a denial, he had snatched her by the arm and dragged her towards the window. She was still blinking in the light when he took her chin and yanked it upwards, at the same time turning the left side of his face towards her.

'You may as well take a good look, so you can tell all your friends what a monster has fed you and sheltered you, and maybe plotted to murder you in your bed.'

It was a painful sight. She could not help flinching, even though she knew he would see her instinctive recoil. The skin across his left cheek was red and bunched. A withered eyelid drooped uselessly over a blind eye.

She had to gather her wits. She had never intended to cause him any distress, she guessed that was the only reason for his anger. His hand seemed very heavy and strong, resting against her neck, his thumb beneath her chin.

'Really, sir, I had no idea — ' Isabel swallowed painfully. Would mentioning his scar only make matters worse?

'So if you had known, you would have respected my privacy and kept away?'

'Yes — no. That's not what I mean either. Please let me explain.'

He let go of her and turned aside.

Dimly, through a mixture of other impressions, Isabel noticed how different his other profile was. The skin was smooth and tight and she guessed he could be no more than ten years older than her. A dark eyebrow was drawn in a frown over a fierce blue eye. His lips were compressed to try to prevent an agitated muscle from twitching in his cheek.

'There is no need to explain. I understand your motives perfectly. I hope you are satisfied with this morning's work.'

Isabel felt like crying, but she knew that wouldn't do a scrap of good. 'You've been so kind to my father. I never meant to upset you. If I can do anything to make amends . . . '

'What exactly do you propose?'

She had no answer to his sarcastic question.

'I suppose there will be one positive outcome from this. I trust you will take care our paths do not cross again while your father is too ill to be moved. Good day, Miss Locke.'

He stepped past her before she could utter a word of protest. She heard him run up the staircase and then a door slam. She considered following him, but what could she say? She could not tell him that his scar didn't matter, because to him clearly it did. Why else would he lock himself away from the world like this?

Her legs were shaking so much, she knew they would not carry her even the relatively short distance back to her room. She staggered towards the great hall instead and pulled one of the heavy, carved chairs away from the dining table, so she could sink into it and cover her face with her hands.

She could see herself through his eyes and it was not a pretty sight. As far as he was concerned, she was a bored, frivolous girl, who wanted to satisfy her curiosity at all costs and would probably tell exaggerated tales about what she had seen. And his poor opinion of her would be justified if he knew how she had pursued him around the garden.

The doctor had told her it would be at least three weeks before her father could endure the shaking of a coach without too much discomfort. That was all the time she had to make her peace with Mr Carwell, if he did not decide to cast them out immediately.

But no, past examples of Mr Carwell's considerateness convinced her he would not expel her father before he was fit to travel. She, however, was another matter. He might suggest to her father that, for the sake of her reputation, it would be better if she returned home, now the immediate danger was past.

She would have to write to him, to say all the things he had not allowed her to say to him face to face. Even if he did not forgive her immediately, maybe in time he would think a little better of her. She would have to coax Mrs Beecroft into helping her, though she was afraid the housekeeper would take

Mr Carwell's part against her.

She merely picked at her breakfast, but her father didn't seem to notice. She considered confiding in him, but she was afraid he would tell her it was her own fault in going against their host's wishes. She had got herself into this mess, and she would try to get out of it without his help.

When she had a moment to spare, she sat down at her desk. But after writing *Dear sir*, she agonised over what to say next. She was not fully satisfied with the finished letter, but she sealed it before going in search of Mrs Beecroft. She did not trust anyone else to deliver the letter directly into Mr Carwell's hands.

'You look pale and tired,' Mrs Beecroft remarked in her usual friendly way when Isabel located her in the housekeeper's room, next to the cloisters. She was sewing a button onto what was obviously her master's coat. 'Is there anything troubling you?'

He hadn't told her. The thought

flashed across her mind like lightning.

'I, I.' How could she make her confession now? 'Would you give this letter to your master? It's very important, you must make sure he reads it. And tell him I am sorry to be such a dreadful imposition.'

Her voice was trembling with unshed tears and she squeezed her eyes shut, reliving the scene that morning.

'I'm sure Mr Carwell wouldn't wish you to feel like a burden.'

Isabel was not so sure after their encounter, but she avoided replying to her remark by saying, 'I'd like to do something to thank him. I'd sketch the house, only my drawing master was never satisfied with my efforts, in fact he told me never to tell anyone that I had been his pupil.'

'I'm sure it can't be as bad as that.'

'Well,' Isabel tugged one of her ringlets dubiously, 'Papa puts my pictures up on the walls, but then, he is my father.'

Mrs Beecroft chuckled and Isabel too, managed a smile. It was strange how such a simple little thing could make her feel better.

'Don't you make anything else for your father?' Mrs Beecroft asked, snipping off her thread and shaking out the coat. A faint trace of Mr Carwell's scent wafted towards Isabel from its heavy folds. How strange that she recognised it, she had not had time to notice it consciously that morning.

'I've embroidered nightcaps and waistcoats for him,' she said doubtfully, 'but Mr Carwell doesn't strike me as the sort of man to care for such frivolous things.'

Mrs Beecroft threw her a sharp look as she draped the coat over the back of a chair, to be put away later. 'You've seen him, then, have you?'

The blood rushed into Isabel's face. 'Yes. I'm afraid I put myself in his way this morning.'

The housekeeper leaned towards her suddenly, both palms pressed to the tabletop. 'He doesn't want your pity, you know.'

'I know. That's why I need your help, because I don't want to make matters worse between us. You know him better than anyone else.'

She didn't reply immediately. Isabel watched her bustling about, picking out a stocking from a tangled pile, finding a darning needle, matching the yarn.

'How long does it take you to make one of those waistcoats for your father?' Mrs Beecroft asked, threading her needle.

'I don't know. I could only work at them now and then, when I wasn't needed elsewhere.'

'Mr Carwell used to be fond of bright waistcoats. His only vanity, I used to call it. Nothing too garish, mind, just a little cheerful.'

'It shouldn't take long if I spend most of my time on it.' Isabel caught herself up short. 'But wouldn't it upset your master, by reminding him of, you know, past times?'

'Come with me,' Mrs Beecroft said, getting up suddenly. 'There's something I want to show you.'

She led the way round the cloisters to a door in the very corner of the building. Here she inserted a large key and applied her shoulder to the door, which had swollen in the damp. Isabel could feel the cold from the flagstones ooze through her shoes.

The room smelt musty, as if nobody had been inside for a long time. It was clearly used for storing things that were rarely used or had seen better days. Mrs Beecroft squeezed past a bulky chest to a draped rectangle propped on a rickety chair.

'He doesn't know I kept this, ordered me to burn it with the lumber,' she said, whisking the old sheet aside. 'That's the only reason I keep this door locked, so he doesn't chance upon it.'

Isabel stared at the object, feeling as if icy water was trickling down behind the neck of her gown. It was the portrait of a young man with symmetrical features, a high forehead and deep blue, intelligent eyes that challenged whoever looked into them. She knew from the first instant who it was.

Mrs Beecroft sighed and rubbed her sleeve solicitously across his face.

'My heart bleeds for him sometimes,' she said. 'I've known him since he was a boy, though I scarcely saw him after the accident, until he came to stay with his dying grandfather. Such a handsome young feller as he was.'

'Yes, he was. He still is, save for that one side of his face.'

'Aye, so I tell him. This is the only picture left from those times, because the old master had it. He destroyed all the others when his marriage, well, never mind about that.'

'I didn't know Mr Carwell had been married.' The words escaped her before she could stop herself.

'He wasn't. That's the tragedy.'

Isabel bit her lips and ducked her head, feeling she had tricked the housekeeper into revealing more than she had intended. Mrs Beecroft sighed as she took one last look at the portrait before covering it up. She tugged the door shut and locked it behind them.

'I'd like something to remind him he is still a young man,' she said. 'I was hoping when you came, silly, really, isn't it?'

'No, it's not silly. I do want to help if I can. Do you really think one colourful waistcoat will do the trick?'

The older woman gave her a conspiratorial smile. 'It can't do any harm.'

Isabel fetched her sketchpad and pencil and they soon had it settled between them. That done, Isabel gathered her possessions to return to her father, but Mrs Beecroft's voice stopped her before she reached the door.

'There's one more thing you can do for the master, if you've a mind.'

'What is it?'

'Leave the window open when you're

practising. I've seen him more than once sitting by an open window or pausing in the garden beneath to listen to the music.'

Isabel blushed, suddenly touched by the image she had conjured up.

But Mrs Beecroft was lost in her own memories. 'He used to have a lovely voice himself,' she said. 'He's never sung since the fire.'

Life at Longwood Priory went on quietly. News came from Squire Davenant that Mr Locke's horse had been recovered at a fair in Leicestershire, but whoever had taken it there to be sold had escaped.

Mr Locke's bruises changed colour and faded and his other injuries began to heal. The doctor allowed him to get up, as long as he did not overexert himself. The broken arm in particular would take a long time to mend.

He tried writing with his left hand, but it was a laborious process and for the most part Isabel acted as his secretary. Every time she picked up a pen, she could not help thinking about Mr Carwell.

He had not replied to her letter. He had sent Mrs Beecroft out of the room before he opened it, so Isabel could not even be sure he had read it. His silence, however, suggested that she had not been forgiven and at times she couldn't help thinking he was being unfair.

She spent every spare moment working on the waistcoat and was astonished at how quickly she proceeded. The back and lining would, of course, be invisible and therefore she left them plain. The design she and Mrs Beecroft had decided on was not extravagant, though elegant enough for Sundays and special occasions.

'If he ever deigned to set foot outside the grounds of this house,' Mrs Beecroft added with a sigh.

Isabel did not forget her other promise either and often played the harpsichord in the library with the window open. The music did not seem so unnaturally loud when she could hear the wind rustling the new leaves and the birds warbling.

One evening, she stayed in the library much longer than usual, going through her entire repertoire before she finally gave up. She closed the lid of the instrument and the window and slowly picked her way along the gallery to her father's room.

Her father looked more alert than he had been for a long time.

'You'll never guess what just happened,' he said.

'What, Papa?'

'Mr Carwell was here. You've only just missed him. He came to apologise for not introducing himself sooner, but he has been very busy, setting the estate to rights — he didn't say so, but I suspect his grandfather had let things slide a little towards the end.'

Isabel smiled, hoping there was a grain of truth in the excuse. She let her father talk without interruption. He seemed much taken with their host, commented on what an intelligent and well-educated young man he was and barely mentioned the scar.

'He wears a black silk patch over his left eye too. It's such a pity such a man has lost part of his sight.'

Perhaps that was why Edmund Carwell had been so agitated and embarrassed that morning, Isabel thought. He had not been wearing the patch. Her heart had quickened at her father's tale, but now it lapsed back into sluggishness. It was clear Carwell had chosen a time when he knew she was occupied and most probably fled as soon as the music stopped.

Following doctor's orders, Mr Locke went to bed almost immediately after supper. Isabel was not sleepy and there was nothing else for her to do, so she sat up and finished the waistcoat. It was dark blue in colour, to match his eyes, with green foliage and yellow flowers embroidered round the buttonholes and along the pocket flaps, and Mrs Beecroft assured her that it would suit him admirably.

She gave it to the housekeeper before

breakfast the following morning, but she had no great hope that anything would be resolved.

There was a letter from Sarah Waite, so while the doctor was examining her father, she decided to read it in the formal garden. Her father was so much better, she hoped they would be able to go home soon. She wanted to return to ordinary life, to walks with Sarah and vague dreams about the dashing Captain Davenant. Strange that she had hardly thought about Kit since she came here. She had been too preoccupied with the mystery of Edmund Carwell.

The letter brought it back so vividly. Sarah was fretting about her costume, since she'd wanted to be something more original than a shepherdess or milkmaid.

I suggested Cleopatra, but Mamma would not hear of it, she wrote. *She said it would not be respectable for an unmarried girl. You know much more about books and history than I do*

— you must think of something.

Homesickness overwhelmed Isabel. If Papa did not get better soon, she might miss the masquerade altogether. And then Captain Davenant's regiment would leave for summer quarters and it might be years before she saw him again.

She was so lost in thought, she did not hear the footsteps until they were close. Assuming it was the doctor come to give her his verdict, she dashed away an incipient tear and turned eagerly in his direction, a dozen questions on her lips. They all froze like icicles as she looked up into the scarred face of Edmund Carwell.

4

There was something stern about the piercing blue eye that was fixed on her. He was wearing the eye-patch this time, his expression unreadable. Was he still angry with her? She looked away, and then was afraid he might think it was because of his scar and turned her eyes back to his face. But she did not want to stare either.

'Miss Locke.'

She could not glean any hints from his studiously neutral tone either, but she curtsied politely. She swallowed and discovered her mouth was dry.

'I was just about to go,' she lied, hastily folding Sarah's letter and pushing it into her pocket.

'Please don't disturb yourself on my account,' he said stiffly. 'I believe I owe you an apology for the way I behaved on the first occasion we met.'

'Think nothing of it,' she replied coolly. If he could not sound any more sincere than that, then he was not worth worrying over.

'However, I cannot accept your gift. I am willing to believe you mean well, but I am not an object of charity or pity.'

'I don't regard you as either,' she flashed back, suddenly angry. 'If you are too proud to wear the waistcoat, give it away to someone who needs it.'

She turned away.

'Don't go, Miss Locke.' In two strides he was by her side. He grasped her arm, but instantly let go again. His voice husky, he went on. 'Perhaps I have been over-sensitive and over-hasty. I wanted to make a good impression, if I ever found the courage to introduce myself, and I was ashamed to let you see me like that.'

Isabel found she was unable to take her eyes off his hands. They were trembling with suppressed emotion, indicating how much this confession cost him. Apparently becoming aware he was betraying himself, he clenched them firmly behind his back, out of sight.

'You shouldn't be ashamed,' she exclaimed. 'The reason why I was so anxious to meet you was because you had left such a good impression already.'

The unscarred side of his face was turned towards her, perhaps to conceal the blemish, or perhaps because that was the only way he could see her properly.

'I'll accept your apology, if you will accept mine,' he said, offering to shake hands.

She slid her hand into his. 'Of course.'

There was a long, awkward pause. Carwell released her hand, each finger opening gradually like a flower uncurling its petals.

'Were you intending to go for a walk?' he asked.

'Later. I have to wait for news from

the doctor first.'

'Ah.'

Isabel guessed he had been about to propose they should go together, but her words made that impossible.

'Perhaps we could sit down for a while in a sheltered nook,' she suggested. 'The wind is rather chill.'

'Certainly.' A little awkwardly, he offered her his arm. Just as awkwardly, she accepted it. To prevent another silence, she asked him the name of an exotic plant. He told her and pointed out another rarity.

'I hope you have not been bored during your stay.'

'Oh no, there has been plenty to occupy me.'

Isabel noticed her companion had begun to breathe faster, as if mustering the courage to say something in particular.

'You are fond of music, I gather?'

'Yes, but it is a little eerie, playing in an empty room like that. I always feel as if I am disturbing the peace.'

'By no means. You must play as often as you like.' The eagerness was audible in his voice and he checked himself.

'Do you like music, too?' Isabel asked, conscious that she must not betray how much Mrs Beecroft had told her.

'Yes, very much. Perhaps you will play for me later?'

'Perhaps,' Isabel agreed, mustering a shy smile and trying out a little joke, 'if you ask me very nicely.'

For a moment his lashes flickered and she was afraid he would misunderstand her. And then a smile spread across his lips, illuminating his face.

'I see you are going to wreak your revenge,' he said. 'I am your most humble servant, madam, and beseech you to grant me this boon, so I may die happy.'

Isabel's laugh rang across the formal garden, echoing as it struck the walls of the house. She clapped her hand to her mouth, afraid she had made too much noise, but before he could reassure her, they were interrupted by a cough.

'Good morning, Miss Locke, Mr Carwell.'

Isabel sprang to her feet. Neither of them had heard the doctor approach.

'How is my father?'

'I think he will be strong enough to bear the journey in a week or so. However ... I may be wrong, but I have the impression Mr Locke is the sort of man who will not sit still for long unless he is compelled to. Isn't that so, Miss Locke?'

'Yes, my father is always busy. There are so many calls on his time.'

More than once her father had suggested having his post forwarded from home, but hitherto the doctor had insisted on absolute rest.

'I would far rather he convalesced a little longer before he throws himself into the bustle of his usual routine.'

'Then don't tell him he is fit enough to travel.' Mr Carwell spoke before Isabel had fully grasped the doctor's meaning. 'I undertake to keep him here for another fortnight or a month, or however long you deem necessary.'

'Oh, but we must be such a burden,' Isabel protested.

'It's one I'm willing to bear.' Carwell turned towards the doctor. 'Don't worry, they cannot leave unless I choose to lend them my carriage.'

'It won't be for more than a fortnight,' the doctor assured them. 'It is better if your father has a long rest, Miss Locke. He is no longer as young as he was, though I daresay, like me, he forgets it most of the time. I'm sure between the two of you, you will be able to keep him entertained.'

Isabel and Edmund Carwell exchanged wry looks. Their peace had been sealed too recently for either of them to be certain of the other's reaction. Then the doctor hinted he wished to speak to Isabel alone, so Mr Carwell promptly excused himself. As they walked back towards the house, the doctor dropped his voice.

'To be perfectly honest, Miss Locke,

you would be doing more than one person a service if you consented to stay. I've never seen Mr Carwell look so animated.'

Isabel felt uncomfortable at being given the credit for this transformation, so she hastened to say, 'I'll do what I can, but please don't expect miracles.'

She saw no more of Mr Carwell that morning, as she was kept busy trying to reconcile her father to the idea of another fortnight of idleness. Their conversation was interrupted when Mrs Beecroft arrived with an invitation for them to dine with her master in the prior's parlour, a small room off the great hall furnished as a dining-room.

The housekeeper gave Isabel a surreptitious wink and Mr Locke was so pleased with the invitation and the implied compliment to himself, that it was only as they were on the verge of leaving their suite that he remembered something.

'I don't suppose I have to warn you not to stare at Mr Carwell, Isabel. He was badly burnt in a fire some years ago.'

'I know, Papa. Mr Carwell and I have met in the garden.'

Isabel wondered if her father knew anything more about the fire, but there was no time to ask. Their host was waiting for them. Isabel could not help glancing at his waistcoat and felt a pang of disappointment to discover it was not the one she had made.

Never had she been so grateful for her father's sociable nature. He talked enough for all three of them and seemed unaware of any awkward pauses. Despite the secluded life he led, Edmund Carwell was well versed in politics from reading newspapers and could debate all the burning issues of the day, like the growing discontent in America.

They retired to the library after dinner at Edmund Carwell's suggestion and Isabel could not overlook the sidelong glance he gave her. She fumbled more with her music than usual, self-conscious because she had an audience, though she had played and sung to more crowded drawingrooms in the past.

'You don't play, do you, sir?'

Isabel was relieved her father put the question instead of her.

'Not any more. But I still enjoy listening to music.'

'It seems I shall have to sing for both our suppers, Papa,' Isabel said with a laugh.

'And if she doesn't do well enough, will we be cast out into the wilderness?' her father asked, glancing at their host.

'Absolutely. So sing, wench, sing.'

Isabel gave them another song, but on the last chord, she happened to glance at Edmund Carwell. He was sitting very still, gazing out of the window at the garden and she was overwhelmed by a sense of his sadness. It was not just the disfiguring scar of his impaired sight that haunted him, she was sure. There was something more, something too deep for words.

* * *

The next ten days passed much more quickly than those that had preceded them. Edmund Carwell was sometimes absent, busy with his own affairs, but he always made a point of dining with his guests. Almost every day he went for a walk with one or both of them, though Mr Locke was still liable to become breathless if he over-exerted himself because his ribs were not fully healed.

Several days of rain put an end to all but the shortest walks. Carwell, feeling he could not desert his guests, spent most of his time with them. He gave Mr Locke complete access to his collection of minerals, ancient coins and other curiosities, some of which had been dug up in the garden of the priory and others purchased during his travels as a young man.

They played chess or cards, or sometimes Mr Carwell put his beautiful voice to good use by reading aloud from the newspaper or a book, while

Isabel sewed and her father rested in a comfortable chair by the fire.

'It's a shame you don't sing any more, sir,' Isabel remarked one day, having caught their host gazing at her with a wistful air. 'We could sing duets. I'm afraid I'm boring you, repeating myself over and over again.'

'You're not boring us,' Carwell assured her, so quickly the words tripped over each other.

'Couldn't you try just one song?' Mr Locke interceded. 'What part did you sing? Tenor?'

'Baritone.' He was frowning, but more in sorrow than in anger, Isabel thought.

'Please won't you try?' she begged.

'My voice must be very rusty.'

'Never mind. My father is a most undiscerning critic.' Isabel could see Carwell was wavering. 'He thinks everything I do is perfect and won't listen to you at all.'

Mr Locke protested vehemently at his daughter blackening his name, but there was a twinkle in his eye. Carwell could not help laughing.

'Very well. It seems I am outnumbered.'

They chose a song together, their heads bent in close proximity over the piles of sheet music. Isabel's heart lurched as she felt his breath ruffle her hair. Being so close to a tall, broadshouldered male body was somehow unsettling.

Carwell cleared his throat nervously as she set the music on the stand. She managed the introduction without stumbling, but almost stopped in amazement when she heard the mellow voice blending with hers. He was a little husky, it was true, especially on the higher notes, but his confidence increased as they went on.

'Bravo!' Mr Locke cried out, jumping to his feet in enthusiasm. 'Encore!'

Isabel glanced at Edmund Carwell over her shoulder. He looked flushed, but there was a gleam in his eye.

'I suppose it can't do any harm to try

one more,' he said.

In the end they sang three or four duets, before Carwell's voice began to crack under the unaccustomed strain.

Edmund Carwell's voice was a little hoarse at breakfast the next morning, and in between eating and drinking, his fingers drummed distractedly on the white damask tablecloth, as if he had no control over them any more. His eye lit up as Isabel took her place beside him, opposite her father. His expression made something contract deep inside her.

In his ordinary tones, he proposed they should take advantage of a dry spell to walk in the garden. Mr Locke excused himself, but Isabel could not resist the lure of the cornflower blue sky.

They walked almost in silence until they reached the orchard. Every tree was full of pink or white blossom and Isabel pulled away from her companion to draw down one delicate, frothy branch.

'You are lucky to live in such a beautiful place,' she said.

He did not reply and she turned around, fearing he had moved on without her and she was talking to herself. But Edmund Carwell stood nearby, watching her intently.

'There are even prettier sights,' he said.

Something in his expression made her flush. Her mind fluttered like a trapped bird, trying to find some way to escape from this situation without offending him. But instead of saying anything more, he moved on a few steps and Isabel lengthened her stride to catch up with him.

'How is your voice today?' she asked, afraid of allowing silence to develop between them. 'I hope you did not overtax it yesterday.'

His expression softened. He was touched by her concern and Isabel bit her lip.

'My throat is a little sore, but it is no great matter. I hope we will be able to try a few more songs this evening.'

Isabel seized on the subject eagerly. And yet the conversation about music fizzled out quickly and soon nothing could be heard but the crunch of footsteps on the gravel.

'I shall miss you when you are gone.'

The soft words squeezed her heart into a knot.

'Perhaps you will permit us to visit you sometimes,' she said, deliberately including her father in her reply.

'I should like that very much,' he replied, but his tone was flat.

'We'll come every week, if you like.'

'Don't make promises you cannot keep.'

'I mean it.'

'I know you do — for now.'

'For always.' She laid her hand tentatively on his arm and he clasped it with his other hand. 'You are welcome to call on us whenever you choose.'

Even as she said the words, Isabel knew it was dangerous to promise so much. If he saw her frequently and brooded on her image when he was alone, it might raise hopes she could not fulfil. Because, no matter how she twisted it around in her mind, she could not imagine marrying Edmund Carwell.

He was close enough to kiss her, she realised suddenly. He only had to dip his head a little lower. His lips moved and his fingers tightened around hers. On impulse, Isabel turned aside and she heard a sharp intake of breath close to her ear.

'I hardly think that would be wise,' he said and she could hear a dangerous edge to his voice. He shook himself free of her grasp. 'Suppose you had visitors? I wouldn't want to frighten women and children into fits.'

'You mustn't say such terrible things. They simply aren't true.' Isabel whipped her head round to fix her eyes on his face, trying to impress her sincerity upon him.

'You flinched from me when you first saw me.'

'I didn't know what to expect.'

'So now I must have a servant to precede me wherever I go to warn strangers about my imminent approach?'

'That is not what I meant and you know it.'

Edmund Carwell had dropped his head and half-turned from her, but his right eye betrayed him. He peeped in her direction, willing her to convince him.

'Maybe ignorant and unkind people will judge you by your appearance, but anyone who takes time to get to know you properly will quickly forget your scar and remember only your warm heart and your intelligence. It's only a tiny part of you that is damaged.'

'I wish I could forget,' he said, touching his left cheek. 'If it were just my appearance, perhaps it would be easier, but there is no way I can escape from my blindness, except in my dreams.'

'You dream you have your sight back?' she asked, shivering at the revelation.

'Yes. I can see so many things all at the same time, and then I wake and find everything dark or distorted . . . '

'And reality is all the harder to bear because of the contrast, like a prisoner dreaming of freedom.'

The expression in his eyes revealed his vulnerability. 'You do understand,' he murmured.

'I am trying to.'

She could see the muscle working in his cheek. His eye stared past her, through the open gates, towards the lake. He shook his head.

'It's no use, Isabel. I am older than you and have more experience. I know you mean to be kind, but as soon as you leave Longwood, I will lose you, slowly, by degrees. You will marry someone else, have children. Perhaps make me the godfather of one of them and then drift farther away from me. I've seen it happen before.'

The sadness in his voice made her want to prove him wrong, to show him he was not as ugly as he felt he was.

'It won't happen this time, I promise.'

He smiled at her, but his gaze was bleak.

'You don't understand. If the woman I was engaged to deserted me, I can hardly expect a mere acquaintance of a few weeks to — ' His voice caught and he compressed his lips to prevent another sound from escaping.

'I'm sorry. I didn't know.'

He seemed so lonely and in need of the touch of another human being. On impulse, she laid her hand against his scarred cheek. It felt softer than she had expected, apart from the hard ridge of his cheekbone beneath her thumb.

He shuddered at her touch and, without warning, she remembered the portrait Mrs Beecroft had shown her. He was older now and suffering had added lines to his face, but he was still a good-looking man.

He raised his hand to cover hers, imprisoning it against his face. Isabel made no attempt to withdraw it. For a long moment he gazed into her eyes. Then he drew her hand down to his lips and pressed a passionate kiss into her palm.

An instant later he sprang back.

'Forgive me,' he gasped and fled. She could still feel the warmth of his lips against her skin.

5

Isabel brooded over the scene in the orchard for hours, her thoughts in turmoil. She blamed herself for encouraging Edmund Carwell, yet she was unable to stop thinking about the sensation of his lips on her hands.

It was not till evening that she found herself momentarily alone with him. Her father expected them to sing together and she could think of no excuse to avoid it. While they were both poring over the music, Carwell took the opportunity to murmur, 'I want to apologise for what happened in the orchard. I lost my head, but it won't happen again.'

Isabel smiled and tried to reassure him, but she felt an odd pang, almost like disappointment.

For the next few days, she felt she was balancing on the brink of a precipice. She knew her behaviour towards Carwell was growing erratic. Even in her father's presence, she was less at ease with him. At first she avoided being alone with him, until she saw the pain in his eye and the proud stiffening of his spine, and then she couldn't help proposing a walk or a game of chess.

His moods seemed to fluctuate as often as hers. At times he locked himself away in his room. Then he would exert himself to entertain his guests, especially Mr Locke. Almost every time she looked up from the harpsichord or her sewing, Isabel caught him watching her. But when they were alone, he was always scrupulously polite and there was no repetition of the scene in the orchard.

A shadow fell across his features when Mr Locke announced one evening that the doctor had declared him sufficiently recovered from his injuries.

'We'll have to start making preparations for our departure.'

'Departure? Oh, ah, yes. You'll stay one more day, won't you? I'm afraid I cannot spare the horses tomorrow.' But although he was apparently addressing Mr Locke, his eyes drifted towards Isabel.

'Well, I have been idle so long, I doubt one day will make any difference,' Mr Locke said with a sigh of mock-resignation.

After breakfast the following day, Isabel supervised the packing. Eliza had sent more clothes when it became clear the Lockes would have to stay at Longwood Priory for some time, but even so the process did not take long. Isabel was half-glad to be going home and half-sorry. She didn't like the idea of leaving Edmund Carwell behind.

The sun was shining. This would be her last chance to walk in the garden, but she was wary of being caught alone by Edmund Carwell. If his resolve were going to crack, it would be now. She realised she didn't want him to propose, because if she rejected him, she would lose him as a friend.

As she stole along the gallery, she could hear her father's voice behind a closed door. Almost certainly Carwell was with him and therefore would be engaged for a while. Long enough at least for her to escape into the wood where she would not be easy to find.

She set out a brisk pace, forcing herself not to run and trying not to look like she was hiding. But she had not quite reached the safety of the tress when she heard the crunch of footsteps behind her.

Pretend you haven't heard. It's probably only one of the servants. She kept her eyes fixed straight ahead, but she was conscious that someone was watching her. Her breath came in sharp bursts, though she was trying to saunter.

She was not left in doubt for long. Rapid steps echoed behind her and a voice, his voice, called, 'Miss Locke!'

Isabel turned. Edmund Carwell was approaching with swift strides and she had time to appreciate how precarious her situation was. If she had stayed in the house, her father would have been present as a witness.

'You were going for a walk?' he asked, as soon as he was within speaking distance.

'Yes.'

'I hope you have no objection to my coming with you?'

'Not at all.' Isabel attempted a smile.

Obviously it was not convincing, since Carwell studied her face and seemed to hesitate before he offered her his arm. She could feel the muscles in his arm were so tight, they quivered with suppressed energy.

'I suppose this will be our last walk together, at least for a while,' he said.

'Yes.' Isabel considered making some remark about the weather but dismissed that as too boring. 'I should like to see the rose garden when it is in full bloom.'

'You are welcome to come and see. I'd promised to take you skating on the lake too, but . . . ' He shrugged.

It wasn't wise to plan too far ahead.

'I'll hold you to that,' she said.

'I almost believe you will. But then, humans seem to have an infinitive capacity for gullibility and self-delusion.'

She realised he was thinking about the woman he had loved and lost. What had she done to hurt him so much that he wouldn't trust anyone any more?

'You shouldn't allow one bad experience to poison the rest of your life. It isn't healthy, locking yourself away like this with nothing but books for company.'

'I'd thank you not to lecture me. You know nothing about me, or my past.'

'No, that's true. But I do know there is hardly anyone who has not been unhappy in love at some point in their life.'

'Tell me, Miss Locke, do you think I was simply unlucky to have been disfigured a week before my wedding? Or maybe you consider I had a timely escape from being saddled with a wife who couldn't love me merely because I had become a hideous, half-blind freak? Perhaps in my circumstances you would be a model of sweetness and patience?'

Isabel was silenced. She had expected this tête-à-tête to be difficult, but she had never intended to quarrel with Carwell on her last day.

'I'm sorry,' he said quietly. 'My temper never used to be so volatile before the fire. I am trying to master it, but you have no idea how hard it is.'

'It's my fault. I had no business prying into your affairs.'

'But I would like to explain, if you will listen.'

Isabel assented, feeling she could do no less. They started walking, but the pace was slow and she felt the fresh breeze seep through her gown, despite the sun peeping through the leaves.

'The fire was in one of my tenant's cottages. It was already fierce by the time I arrived and I was told there was a baby still inside in his cradle.'

'So you went in to find him?'

Carwell nodded, screwing up his eye.

'It was like plunging into hell. Outside you could see the flames and the billowing smoke, but when I got inside, there was nothing but hot, smothering blackness. I still have nightmares about stumbling through that choked cloud, feeling flames all around me, splintering wood, shattering glass . . . And then I staggered against the cradle and it was empty. I couldn't believe it. I rumpled the blankets and began searching the room, although I knew the baby was too young to crawl. I couldn't breathe, Isabel, but I thought I was a failure because I couldn't find that little boy.'

Isabel uttered a murmur of sympathy. It seemed incongruous to be talking about such things on such a beautiful day.

'They told me afterwards that if I'd been farther from the door, they would never have got me out alive. I don't remember that, being brought out, I mean. The last thing I recall was a splintering sound above me and something crashing down around my head.'

'And the baby?' Isabel asked.

'It seems the maidservant had got him, but his mother didn't know and she lost her head when she couldn't find him in the confusion.'

'Thank goodness for that,' Isabel murmured. 'You shouldn't be ashamed of your scars. You are a hero.'

'A hero? I didn't save anyone.'

'But you wanted to, you tried to. How many other people were there who didn't even try to reach the baby? Surely your betrothed realised that?'

Carwell would not look at her. They had come to a clearing where the trees had been cut away to reveal a distant view of the house and he fixed his good eye on that.

'Yes. To do her justice, Anne said all those things. She sat by my bedside while I slid in and out of consciousness and coughed blood. I was swathed in bandages for weeks and she would scold me for scratching my blisters and tried to console me on the first day the doctor removed the padding from my eye and I realised I had lost the sight in it. She even suggested we should get married by special licence while I was still on my sickbed, but I didn't want her to remember our wedding like that.'

'So what went wrong?'

Carwell raised his left hand to his cheek, the long, sensitive fingers running over the puckered skin.

'It was a gradual process. I was incapacitated for a long time with my injuries and not easy to live with. I was often frustrated and angry because I had to learn to adapt, to judge distances — oh, many little things.

'Anne bore it for as long as she could, but she kept deferring our wedding, and in the end I saw how unhappy I was making her and set her free.'

'Are you sure she wanted to be set free?' Isabel asked. Perhaps it was not yet too late, her mind whispered. Perhaps she could find this mysterious

Anne and reunite her with Edmund Carwell. And yet the thought of them living happily ever after gave her a strange pang. Envy, she supposed, since there seemed to be no prospect of a happy ending for herself.

'She's married,' Carwell replied in flat tones. 'She became engaged a month after I released her from our engagement.'

He tugged Isabel's arm to make her face him, as if his next words were of paramount importance.

'I could see as soon as the bandages were removed that Anne recoiled from the scar. She tried to conceal it, of course, but I found myself saying things that I knew would drive her away, even though I wanted her to stay. Towards the end, she could hardly bring herself to look at me. She would never have touched my face as you did.'

The precipice seemed to open up under her feet, cracks spreading ominously around her. I can't marry him. I'm not as good as he thinks I am. I don't know him well enough. I don't love him enough.

'So now you know why I'm not married,' Carwell said, releasing her and uttering a sardonic laugh that did not conceal his true feelings. 'What is your excuse for remaining single?'

Isabel dropped her head. 'Oh, that's simple enough. Papa lost a good deal of money some years ago and my fortune is not large enough to tempt anyone with dependents.'

'But a man of independent means might expect serious consideration?'

Isabel's head dropped even lower. It was perfectly clear what he meant, though etiquette insisted that she should pretend not to understand unless he said something unequivocal.

What should she do? If she hinted he might make an offer, it would suggest he stood a good chance of being accepted. All the usual excuses and delaying stratagems came to her.

But Carwell would interpret anything she said as a rejection solely because of his appearance. She liked him very much, she would miss him when she was gone, but she did not feel for him the same quickening of her pulse that she felt whenever she glimpsed Kit Davenant.

And there was his way of life to consider. Would he expect his wife to stay with him, seeing no friends, going to no public or private gatherings? Or would husband and wife lead separate lives, she flitting about like a butterfly while he waited for her at home?

Isabel swallowed. There seemed to be something sharp caught at the back of her throat, like a burr.

'I, I don't know what to say,' she began, but he interrupted impetuously.

'I know we have only known each other a short time. I know I am maimed and lead an unnatural life. I would not expect you to bury yourself alive in the country for my sake ... ' His voice trailed away. 'No, I am a fool even to dream of such a thing. I knew from the start it was hopeless, and still I allowed myself to grow too attached. I'm sorry. I won't inflict any more protestations of love on you.'

He could not conceal his sorrow and Isabel found words on her lips she had never intended to utter, asking him to change his mind, almost begging him to marry her. Just to prove to him he was not unlovable.

But still the wild bird beat in the cage of her mind. I cannot marry him out of pity. It would be throwing away my life. And he would not thank her for it when he found out. Because, sooner or later, he would find out, she had no doubt about that. He was too intelligent to be deceived for long, and she too bad a liar.

'I'm flattered, of course, sir,' she began. He flinched at the conventional words, but she went on. 'No, let me finish. I've grown very fond of you in the last weeks, but . . . '

'Fond? That's a pretty word since it comes from your lips. No, don't say another word. I am content with your friendship.' Without warning, he lifted her hand to his lips, kissed it hastily and plunged into the darkness of the woods.

Isabel suddenly felt very lonely, unnerved by the stillness. It must have been close to midday and no bird sang. Only the leaves rustled, whispering secrets. She was almost running by the time she burst into open sunshine again and hardly able to breathe.

Isabel did not see Carwell again until dinner. Mr Locke's presence eased some of the awkwardness between the younger pair, but the musical evening was much more of a struggle than on previous days. Carwell was abrupt, as if he was embarrassed at having revealed too much, or perhaps because he was trying to hide his emotion.

When the time came for them to part for the might, Carwell took a solemn farewell of both his guests, wishing them a safe journey. He gave Isabel a long look as he took her hand, but he made no attempt to kiss it.

She hardly expected to see him again

before they left. She was wrong, however. Their host breakfasted with them and made a point of assisting Isabel into the carriage. She felt a momentary pressure from his hand, then it was withdrawn, the steps were folded away, the door shut, and they were on their way home.

6

'Come and sit down,' Sarah Waite said. 'It feels like you've been gone for an age.'

Isabel herself was surprised by how little the parsonage had changed in her absence. The only novelty was Sarah's companion. Kit Davenant had been sitting beside her on the sofa, his body inclined towards her, and their faces still bore the vestiges of conspiratorial grins.

'We were just wondering if you would be home in time for the masquerade,' he said with a meaningful smile and a gallant bow.

Sarah uttered a gurgle of laughter. 'We're preparing a surprise for you and everyone else,' she said, ignoring Kit's mock-serious attempts to silence her. 'It would be such a coup if we could manage it.'

'How intriguing. Will you give me a clue?'

But neither of them would tell her any more, both incoherent with suppressed laughter. Isabel tried to smile. She felt excluded and hurt, but she could hardly reproach her friend in front of the captain. A moment later she wished they had continued their mysterious hints.

'Your turn,' Sarah said. 'You must tell us about Mr Carwell. What is he like?'

'Yes, do tell, Miss Locke,' Kit urged her. 'What is the great mystery?'

Isabel was aware that her last letter from Longwood had been much more reticent than the first, which had described the house and the mysterious half-glimpses of Mr Carwell. But when she finally met him, it had seemed wrong to say too much about him to a gossip like Sarah, knowing how much he valued his privacy. Isabel racked her brains and prayed for an intervention.

'There's nothing much to tell. Mr Carwell is a perfect gentleman.'

'Oh, Bel, don't be so boring. There must be more to it.' Sarah's tea was getting cold in its little porcelain cup, but she did not seem to care. 'Is it true he hates all his fellow creatures?'

'Indeed it is not.' Isabel could hardly contain her indignation. 'He was very generous. As for why he prefers a quiet life, well, that is his own business. If you can keep secrets, so can I.'

'Hey-day, madam,' Sarah exclaimed. 'Anyone would think you were in love.'

Isabel denied it vehemently, blushing as she became aware Kit was watching them in amusement.

But Sarah merely chuckled. 'Methinks the lady doth protest too much.'

After several more minutes of teasing, Kit took pity on Isabel and turned the conversation back to the masquerade. He begged Sarah to tell him about her costume and made some wild guesses, but she ridiculed all his suggestions with an arch smile.

He said far less to Isabel, but there was something in the way he looked at her that made her heart flutter. And yet, every now and then, the memory of Edmund Carwell flitted across her mind, like a shadow across the sun.

Once Davenant had gone, Sarah turned to Isabel eagerly.

'What on earth am I going to do about my costume?' she wailed. 'I've looked into every book in Papa's study and I'm at my wits' end.'

'You mean you still have not thought of anything?' Isabel asked, exasperated. 'After everything you said to Captain Davenant?'

'Oh, don't preach. Have you decided what you're going to wear?'

'I'll probably go as a domino,' Isabel muttered.

Sarah, in addition to her quarterly allowance, had begged funds from her married siblings, and even her father had contributed a little extra, when his wife's attention was distracted. Isabel had no such resources and money was tighter than ever since her father had been unable to work. She supposed the nondescript costume of a domino, a hooded cloak and a mask to be worn over her best gown, would be cheap and not much trouble.

Sarah pulled a face. 'You have no imagination.'

'Your imagination hasn't got you very far either,' Isabel pointed out, peeping over her friend's shoulder at the blank sheet of paper on which she had been meant to sketch her costume. 'What about a character from Shakespeare, like Juliet or Cordelia?'

'How would anyone know who I was meant to be?' Sarah made a few vague strokes on the paper, then sat back and tapped her pencil meditatively against her lips. 'I could go as Viola or Rosalind, dressed as a boy.'

'No! Can you imagine your mother consenting to anything so outrageous?'

'Real actresses do it,' Sarah muttered sulkily.

'I know!' Isabel suddenly cried out, realising what they reminded her of. 'Why don't you go as Ophelia, decked in flowers, talking nonsense with your usual insane glint in your eyes?'

Sarah threw herself into the idea with enthusiasm, enlisting Isabel and her mother to help with the costume, while insisting upon absolute secrecy. Mrs Waite was a little dubious at first about letting her daughter play a madwoman all night, but, as Sarah pointed out, it would be such a pretty costume and so virginal.

A week flew by. Isabel spent all her spare time making false flowers for Sarah from scraps of silk. She saw a good deal of Kit Davenant too. He called at Mr Locke's house and the parsonage, and she and Sarah came across him on their walks far too frequently for it to be an accident. He bantered with them both, but his eyes often lingered on Isabel.

She also made time to accompany her father to Longwood Priory. It felt like stepping into a completely different world after the whirl of activity at home. The stillness was soothing, and yet she felt a weight of sadness settle on her like snow on an evergreen at the thought that she would have to leave soon.

Edmund Carwell came out on to the steps to greet them. His smile and the brilliant sunshine illuminated his face, emphasising his superb bone structure.

Inevitably the conversation over tea and cakes turned to the masquerade. Since Edmund Carwell was a recluse, she didn't think it would do any harm to tell him about Sarah's costume, though she had to swear her father to secrecy, on pain of death.

'You would have made a pretty Ophelia yourself, I fancy,' Carwell remarked with a glance that made Isabel blush. 'Unless you have a better idea for your own costume?'

'No, I'm not much good at playacting. I could never sustain a role for the whole evening like Sarah Waite.' Isabel seized on the first excuse she could think of. She couldn't talk about money to this man of all men. 'I'm perfectly happy being a domino.'

She changed the subject hastily, but throughout the rest of the visit, she found Carwell's eyes resting on her thoughtfully, as if he was brooding on something.

And so it proved the following day. Captain Davenant had stepped in, ostensibly to make certain Isabel was going to attend a musical party at the parsonage in two days' time, when there was a knock at the front door. A moment later Eliza appeared.

'There's a parcel arrived for you, Miss Locke.'

'For me? I wasn't expecting anything.'

'There's a letter, too.'

Eliza held it out, but somehow Kit Davenant plucked it out of her hand before Isabel could take it.

'A gentleman's hand if I am not mistaken,' he murmured in Isabel's ear as he passed it to her. 'Is there something the gossips ought to know?'

Isabel flushed. She had only seen the

handwriting a few times, but she knew it at a glance. It was a breach of etiquette for Carwell to write to her like this, and even worse to send a present. But worst of all was that it had happened in front of Kit Davenant.

'Only an old uncle.' Her voice came out in a croak. 'My godfather.'

It was the only thing she could think of. She glanced up at the officer and found a gently mocking smile on his lips. Clearly he did not believe her.

'I'm sure he must be very fond of his little goddaughter,' he remarked, but taking pity on her, he bid her farewell and departed.

Isabel watched him go from the window. She didn't know whether to cry or scream with frustration. She wanted to tear up the letter and send back the package unopened. She never wanted to see Edmund Carwell again. He had ruined everything. Kit would think she was a woman of loose morals, or perhaps that she was secretly engaged.

Isabel hurtled up the stairs to her room, the letter still crumpled in her hand. But she was brought up short at the door. A parcel, much larger than she had expected, had been placed on her bed. There was no escape.

Angrily she tore at the paper, nearly ripping the letter in two as she broke the seal.

Dear Miss Locke,

I know I am taking a great liberty, but I hope you will forgive a well-meaning friend. I could not bear to think of you expending so much time to help your friend with her costume that you have no time for your own.

The paragraph calmed her a little. Carefully she put the letter down, so she could wipe the moisture from her eyes and take a deep breath.

Perhaps I ought to explain, Carwell went on, *that I belong to a family where nothing is ever thrown away if it might be useful. The gown I am sending you belonged to my grand-mother many years ago. I read somewhere that it is fashionable in London to go to masquerades dressed as a Van Dyke portrait and thought perhaps this might do. Mrs Beecroft, the only person I have consulted on this matter, says she believes it will only need a few minor adjustments to fit you.*

If you cannot bring yourself to accept the gown as a gift, please consider it as a loan. I hope you will condescend to wear it, though I will understand if you decide it is too old, or that I have been too forward in offering it to you.

Your humble and obedient servant,

Edmund Carwell.

Isabel sat absolutely still for what seemed like an eternity, the letter resting on the dressing-table before her. She was touched by his thoughtfulness.

Nevertheless, she was sure that accepting the gown, even as a loan, must be improper. She would have to ask her father, and yet she doubted he was an authority on correct behaviour in young ladies. And he did not know that Carwell had half-proposed to her.

She shouldn't even open the parcel. But curiosity plucked at her. Perhaps the gown would be hideous. Perhaps it would be too musty or completely the wrong size and she would have a legitimate reason to send it back with the prettiest letter she could contrive.

She unfastened the cord around the box and lifted its lid. The musky smell of old perfume somehow made her think of the wings of long-dead moths. But as she folded back the sheets of paper with which the box was lined, her breath caught.

Her fingers trembling, Isabel lifted out a shimmering gown of midnight blue silk, apparently unfaded by age. It ran through her fingers like water as she unfolded it. She couldn't help herself.

She took it by the shoulders and held it against her as she turned to the mirror. She recognised its plunging neckline and full, elbow-length sleeves from one of the portraits in the drawing-room at Longwood. The colour suited her, making her hair look almost fair.

It must be precious to have been preserved all this time. How could she possibly accept it? Carefully she folded the gown and placed it back in the box, but several times before her father returned home for dinner, she went back to peep at it again.

As she had half-anticipated, her father thought she was making a fuss about nothing and ought to accept Edmund Carwell's generous offer.

'What harm can it possibly do?'

Isabel didn't dare answer. Obviously it had never crossed his mind that Carwell might be in love with her and that he might think she returned his feelings if she borrowed the gown.

At her father's instigation, she tried it on. Isabel's last hope lay in the possibility that it might not fit, but that too was dashed to pieces. It was a little loose at the bosom and tight at the waist, but otherwise it fitted perfectly.

'We'll hang it out to air a bit,' Eliza said, fussing with a ruffle at the neck to make it fall correctly, 'and tease your hair into ringlets, and all the gentlemen'll be swooning at your feet.'

Isabel could see herself gliding into the Davenants' drawing-room as heads turned in her direction and Captain Davenant could not take his eyes off her all night.

Without warning, a dart of pain shot through her and she felt ashamed of using one man's gift to seduce another. But, guilty or not, she knew there was no power on earth that could make her send the gown back. She wanted it too badly.

★ ★ ★

Isabel soon had cause to regret her decision. At the musical party, while most of the young people were gathered in a merry knot around the harpsichord, Mrs Waite drew her aside and asked her if it was wise to go on visiting Mr Carwell.

'I know your father is present and nothing improper could happen, but other people are not so generous-minded. I've even heard some suggest that your father is trying to make a match between you and Mr Carwell, purely for mercenary reasons.'

'That's not true. Who told you that?'

'Don't fret your head about that, child. The main thing is to avert trouble as soon as possible. They'll soon find someone else to gossip about.'

The little conversation lingered in her mind, spoiling her enjoyment. Before Mrs Waite had summoned her to her side, Kit Davenant had been beside her, so close they were nearly touching and she could feel his breath on her cheek.

But after Mrs Waite's warning, everything seemed poisoned. It struck her that Sarah was behaving oddly, laughing too loudly and answering Isabel's remarks more sharply than usual. There was something cold about the way she pecked at Isabel's cheek when they said goodbye and the strange phenomena troubled her so much that she scarcely noticed that Kit murmured a compliment in her ear as he helped her with her cloak.

Afterward, as she lay awake in bed, she thought of a dozen things she ought to have said. Kit would think her dull and it wouldn't matter how beautiful her costume was because he would find someone more interesting.

And what was she to do about Edmund Carwell? She couldn't abandon him without a word, after he had been so kind to her. It would be confirming his worst fears about human nature. The very thought of never seeing him again was more painful than she had expected. If only it were possible to meet him casually in public, to maintain their friendship without all this petty gossip.

There was nothing for it. She would have to go to Longwood one last time and try to explain. But she was not at all sure Edmund Carwell would understand.

7

It was all very well taking such a decision, but she was forced to defer putting it into action. The days between Mrs Waite's warning and her next visit to Longwood were not happy ones for Isabel. Sarah was inexplicably cool and monosyllabic towards her, except for sporadic intervals when she was her usual self, and though Kit Davenant was more attentive than ever, she could not shake off her feelings of guilt.

Edmund Carwell was awaiting for them at the door as he hurried to help Isabel descend from the carriage. The gleam of happiness in his eyes made her feel she was the lowest creature in earth.

Gloom hung over her throughout the visit and the puzzled looks Carwell threw her only made her feel worse. When he sat down on the sofa beside her, her heart fluttered and she had to resist the impulse to clasp his hand to reassure him.

He was beginning to grow wary, his lips tightening as if he knew something unpleasant would follow. He probably thought her fickle, already tiring of her new friend now that he was no longer a mystery to her.

'Is anything wrong, Miss Locke?'

She flushed at his question. 'I — I have a headache,' she lied.

'Perhaps a walk in the fresh air might improve it,' Carwell suggested.

He seemed so concerned about her, she didn't know how to refuse. A private talk was essential, if she wanted to carry out her appointed task, and yet she shrank from it. Did she really have to give up visiting him? Mr Locke had apparently noticed nothing, immersed in studying a large piece of pottery, which has been recently dug out of the priory gardens, so they had the perfect excuse to leave him alone.

The first buds had appeared in the

rose garden. The wind was boisterous without being cold and the skies were clear. But none of it had the power to raise Isabel's spirits.

'Now,' he said quietly, 'why don't you tell me the truth? Is there any way I can help you?'

'You have been too generous already.' She screwed up her eyes to shut out the look of pain she knew would appear on his face as she uttered the next words. 'But I won't be able to visit you any more. They're beginning to gossip about me, to say I am a fortune hunter.'

'So soon?' Isabel was startled by the bitterness of his laugh. 'I thought our friendship would last a little longer than this.'

'It's not all my fault. If I am ever to be married, my reputation must be spotless.'

Abruptly he turned away from her and wrenched a bud from its spray, uttering a hiss of pain as he did so.

'Did you hurt yourself? Let me see.'

Isabel took his hand between hers,

despite his resistance. She prised out a thorn and a ruby bead gathered on the tip of his finger. His silence unnerved her. She felt his breath quicken on her forehead. Glancing up, she was mesmerised by the blue eye fixed on her face. The muscle was working in his cheek and she had to resist the urge to stroke it into stillness.

'I ought to return the gown too,' she faltered.

'You can't, you mustn't.' There was a wild glint in his eye. 'You've not told anyone where it came from, have you?'

'No, but . . . '

The outermost petal of the rosebud gently touched her lips, stopping her words.

'Then there's no reason to send it back. I want you to have it. You can pretend you've owned it for a long time or that it was a present from an elderly relative.'

He brought himself up short, aware of the desperation in his voice. She had been right then. He had interpreted her acceptance of the gown as a sign of hope.

She dropped her head and the rosebud brushed lightly across her mouth and cheek. She wished she had never said anything. Why couldn't she have ignored the gossip?

'It's not that I don't like you, you must believe that. If we could meet publicly . . . '

The rose was still resting against her cheek, but his hand shook. A dewdrop spilled over its lip and ran down her face like a tear.

'Forgive me,' he said, tilting the rosebud away from her face and brushing the back of the same hand across her cheek. It felt cold against her flushed skin. Isabel shivered. She found herself willing him to fight for her, to use every means to persuade her to change her mind. If he had tried to kiss her, she would not have resisted.

Instead he tried to pull away and she instinctively tightened her grip on his hand. One twist of the wrist and

Edmund Carwell was crushing her hand in his, gazing at her as if trying to fix her face in his memory.

'You promised you wouldn't abandon me and I let myself believe you. I never felt lonely till you were gone. I was happy here alone, or content at least, and you spoilt that.'

She wanted to cover her face, but he would not release her hands. She did not deserve to be happy. It would serve her right if Kit never proposed. And if he did, she ought to refuse.

'I'm sorry, I'm sorry.'

He uttered a groan as she began to sob, her chin lowered to her breast in a vain attempt to hide her face. If this was the right thing to do, why did she feel so awful?

'Oh, God, Isabel, I never meant to make you cry. I take back everything I said.' He let go and while she was still fumbling for a handkerchief, he put his own in her hands. 'I'd no right to make you feel worse than you already do. I shouldn't have tried to buy your affection.'

Isabel protested, but from clear blue skies, a raindrop spattered on her gown, followed by another and another. Carwell snatched her hand and began to run, dragging her along behind him. He yanked open the door and let her in first.

Holding out the rose, he said, 'I meant to give this to you sooner.'

'Thank you.'

Their fingertips met for a moment, emitting a spark. Again, for just a second, she thought he might stoop to kiss her. Abruptly Edmund Carwell turned away.

'I'll tell your father your headache is worse and order the carriage.'

His brusqueness was almost enough to bring back her tears, but she swallowed them down. After all, she had only herself to blame for the desolation in her heart.

★ ★ ★

Edmund Carwell haunted her. Knowing she would never see him again made her dwell on his image. Alone, scarred, trying to resume his old routine — how could she desert him like that? Maybe he, like her, took solitary walks, or sat for hours staring sightlessly out of windows, or did not notice until it was too late that someone had been talking to him.

Kit Davenant exerted all his skill to make her laugh, but lately Isabel had started to notice his faults. There was something self-satisfied about him. She caught him more than once admiring himself in the mirror. When she tried to talk to him seriously about the situation in America, he laughed it off.

'I'll see you come to no harm,' he said, as if she was afraid of heavens knows what. Isabel noticed quivering fans and watchful eyes wherever she went. Women with marriageable daughters had grown up sharp with her. She suspected they only invited her to parties because they thought they would persuade Captain Davenant to come too.

It ought to have been flattering, but something in Kit's manner struck her as false. Isabel tried avoiding him, but the general circle in the town was small and officers' duties were light during peacetime. When she heard that his regiment was to be sent north soon after the masquerade, she felt relieved.

The breach in friendship with Sarah remained unhealed. Sarah seemed wretched much of the time, and then burst into wild parodies of her usual high spirits, but she wouldn't tell Isabel what was wrong.

Two days before the masquerade, when Kit and Isabel met her while out walking, she snubbed them by pretending not to see them. Isabel turned her head over her shoulder to watch Sarah's retreat. Her steps flagged and she accidentally dragged on Kit's arm.

'Don't fret about Miss Waite,' he said. 'She'll come to her senses sooner or later.'

'I don't know what I've done to upset her,' Isabel confessed. 'Sarah was never one to hold grudges.'

'Perhaps there is more to the situation than meets the eye.' The smug grin that was beginning to annoy Isabel was on his lips again.

'What do you mean?' she demanded, lifting her chin in an effort to look haughty, though she was almost sure he could hear the nervousness in her voice.

'I don't profess to be in Miss Waite's confidence, but,' he paused deliberately to tantalise her, 'don't you think it's possible that she might be, well, a little jealous?'

'Jealous? Why?'

The words had hardly escaped her lips when she realised what Kit was hinting at. Sarah was in love with him and she, supposedly Sarah's best friend, had been unaware of it. It seemed obvious now. The light-hearted letters Sarah had written to her while she was away, Kit's constant presence at the parsonage, the way Sarah had bantered with him on that first day after Isabel's return from Longwood . . .

Longwood. The name clanged in her head like a funeral bell. Would she ever see it again? She longed for the wooded paths, the decaying splendour of the formal garden, the quiet afternoon in the library. But most of all, she longed for Edmund Carwell.

Before she could grasp the implications of this revelation, Kit went on, 'Why indeed, Miss Locke? You and I know our friendship is perfectly innocent,' he said, gazing at her with devastatingly seductive eyes that contradicted his words, 'but Miss Waite is still very young.'

Why do I feel nothing? Isabel wondered. She had dreamed about Kit Davenant since she was little more than a child and had always thought a moment like this would be the summit of happiness. Now, in a flash of insight, Isabel realised that her friendship with Sarah was far more important to her than her infatuation with Kit.

With this in mind, she set out for the parsonage after dinner. Even before she reached the front door, she could hear Sarah's voice in the garden. She wouldn't give her a chance to send a message, saying she was not at home. But Isabel was stopped short at the corner of the house by a second voice. A feeling of dread gripped her stomach.

'I thought you would be pleased that Miss Locke and I had made friends. You talked so much about her while she was away.'

'Yes, of course,' Sarah replied, but Isabel could hear suppressed tears in her voice. 'Only the gossips say . . . '

'I thought you were too intelligent to pay any heed to gossip.' Kit's voice grew lower, more seductive. 'I thought we understood each other better than that, Sarah.' He breathed her name softly, caressing it.

Isabel heard no more. She fled. Taking refuge in the graveyard, she leaned against the wall, breathing deeply. Kit had lied to her. His relationship with Sarah was obviously closer than he had led her to believe. The question was — was he merely toying with Sarah, as he had toyed with her, or was he in earnest this time? Was it her duty to warn Sarah before it was too late?

★ ★ ★

Isabel had not told her father about Mrs Waite's warning or the scene in the rose garden with Edmund Carwell. When Mr Locke announced his intention of calling at Longwood Priory on the day before the masquerade, Isabel begged him to excuse her from going.

Mrs Waite had invited her to dine at the parsonage, because Sarah needed help to finish her costume. But a feeling of emptiness overwhelmed Isabel as she watched her father ride off without her.

She was surprised to discover she was the only guest at the parsonage. She knew she was not very good company. She was dreading having to talk to

Sarah. Nor could she prevent herself from brooding about Edmund Carwell, wondering what he was thinking and how he felt about her absence. Perhaps he didn't think about her at all.

The reason for Mrs Waite's invitation became obvious when she contrived to leave the two young women alone after dinner, stitching wreaths of flowers to Sarah's white gown. There was an awkward silence after the door shut.

'I — I wanted to ask you something. You needn't answer, if you don't want to,' Isabel said.

Sarah paled in spite of herself. 'Go on,' she said, dubiously.

'Are you in love with Kit Davenant?'

'No, of course not,' Sarah replied, with a hysterical laugh and a fierce blush.

It was all the answer Isabel needed. 'You know, those rumours about him and me aren't true. I'm not in love with him, and if you were, I wouldn't stand in your way.'

Sarah stared for a long minute at her

sewing. She wouldn't retract her denial, so Isabel blundered on. 'The only thing is, I think you should tread carefully. I'm not sure Kit is a marrying man.'

'Oh, now we come to the truth.' Sarah took fire at once. 'You want to warn me off, so you can keep him for yourself.'

Isabel was appalled. This was just the turn of events she had dreaded.

'No, no, you're wrong. I would love to see you happily married. But I don't want you to be hurt by an accomplished flirt.'

'He's not like that,' Sarah protested, a not of desperation in her voice.

'I hope you're right. Please, Sarah, we've been friends far too long to let a mere man come between us.'

Her face crumpled. 'I'm sorry, Bel. I've behaved appallingly these past weeks. Are you really not in love with him?'

'I wouldn't marry Kit Davenant if he asked me a thousand times. I'm in love with somebody else and I've driven him away,' Isabel said suddenly.

'You're not saying that to make me feel better?'

'I wouldn't lie to you about something so important.'

That broke the ice. By the time Mrs Waite returned, Sarah was chattering to a subdued Isabel as if there had never been a breach in their friendship.

Mr Locke had just returned from Longwood when Isabel got home. She questioned him about his visit, but his answers were disappointingly vague.

The only hint Isabel gleaned was not encouraging. Apparently Mrs Beecroft had confided in her father that her master spent every waking moment improving the estate, supervising repairs himself and poring over plans late into the night.

Knowing Edmund was overworking to bury his unhappiness would make it even harder to enjoy the masquerade. But he had sent the dress. He wanted her to go. She ought to make an effort.

She kept her curlpapers in all day

and she couldn't help feeling a shiver of excitement as she sat in front of the mirror, watching Eliza tease her hair into shape. She was already wearing the matching petticoat of the blue dress and her best pair of silk shoes.

8

It was like stepping into an alien world. Isabel had been to assemblies and parties before, but she was sure she had never seen so many candles lit all at once. The golden light rippled whenever a draught made each flame dance in turn. The chandelier twinkled in rainbow colours, so brightly it almost hurt her eyes.

Amid the banks of hothouse flowers and swags of drapery, strange creatures moved — peasants and slave girls, hussars and sultans, harlequins and columbines, nuns with jewelled habits and characters from plays, novels and folk stories. Dominoes of both sexes and every colour — blue, black, red, pink, white, mingled with the others, anonymous and somehow aloof.

Out of the corner of her eye, Isabel thought she saw a head turn in her direction. She heard a fan flick open and two voices murmuring, but she was far too agitated to be able to tell if they were talking about her.

With relief, she caught sight of Sarah and smiled. Beneath her half-mask, Sarah's lips twitched in reply, but there was no gleam in her eyes and she hastily looked away, scanning the room for somebody else.

Isabel was hurt. Had Sarah forgotten their reconciliation already? And then, as Sarah accosted a female domino with a wildly garbled variation of Ophelia's ravings, Isabel realised what had happened. Sarah had not recognised her because she did not expect to see her in this dress.

With a little gentle pressure on her father's elbow, she managed to steer him in Sarah's direction. They were just in time to hear her take her farewell by exclaiming, 'Goodnight, sweet ladies, goodnight, goodnight.'

'How now, fair Ophelia,' Mr Locke said, intercepting her. 'Dost thou not know us?' He, like most of the older people, had not bothered with a costume.

'There's rosemary, that's for remembrance.' Sarah began picking over her bouquet, but she slid a cunning look at Isabel.

'Alas, poor thing, she's mad,' Isabel chimed in, in theatrical tones.

'Pansies, that's for thoughts, oh, botheration.' Sarah switched to her usual energetic tones. 'You knocked the rest clear out of my head, and such a pretty speech it was too. Is that really you, Isabel Locke? Where on earth did this finery come from?'

'It was lent to me by a friend,' Isabel began, but, apparently ignoring her, Sarah placed her hand on Mr Locke's arm and told him in an earnest tone, 'The Thane of Fife had a wife, where is she now?'

'That's Macbeth, unless I am very much mistaken,' he replied with a laugh. He withdrew to the card-room presently, leaving them alone.

131

'You are a dark horse, keeping this secret,' Sarah chided, testing the quality of her sleeve between her fingers.

Isabel decided against pointing out that they had not exactly been friendly in the last weeks.

'Well, you and Captain Davenant have been keeping secrets from me. I thought I'd have my revenge.' She glanced round the crowded room. 'Have you seen him yet?'

She was not sure how she should react to Kit when, inevitably, they would meet.

'We have conversed,' Sarah replied with uncharacteristic dignity, then burst into giggles. 'You'll see him when he dances the first minuet with whoever his precious mamma deems suitable — there he is, in the hussar's coat with the frogged front and the fur around the collar and cuffs.'

Isabel followed the direction of Sarah's nod and caught sight of a gallant figure kissing the hand of one of the numerous shepherdesses, though this one seemed to have plenty of jewels sewn to her stomacher, and full petticoats.

Her eye was caught by another figure beyond Kit. It was a domino in a black cloak and a deathly white mask, but what distinguished him amid the bustle was his stillness. He was leaning against the wall, watching the company and making no apparent effort to engage anyone in conversation. Isabel saw someone approach him, but when she glanced back a few minutes later, the black domino was once more alone.

She considered asking Sarah if she knew who he was, but Kit Davenant and his partner, the shepherdess, were taking their places for the first minuet.

She had little time to brood. The richness of her gown and the unusualness of Sarah's costume attracted a lot of attention, particularly from the gentlemen. But as she waited for the musicians to tune their instruments for the first country dance, she noticed the black domino again.

He stood in the darkest corner of the room, firelight dancing eerily across the expressionless mask. He had neither asked anyone to dance, nor moved to the card room, as most of the others had done, and she was almost sure his eyes had been turned in her direction. There was something familiar about him, though she could not say what.

When the dancing broke up for supper, Isabel discovered she was not the only one to have noticed the black domino. No-one seemed to know who he was and supper had been anticipated with a good deal of excitement, because in order to eat, a partial unmasking was inevitable.

The usual order of precedence was forgotten, the ladies sitting wherever they could find a seat and the gentlemen standing behind them, so Isabel found herself farther up the table than usual. Much to everyone's chagrin, the black domino politely declined all food, though he was attentive to the needs of the ladies nearest to him.

'A queer fish,' one of the gentlemen remarked in Isabel's hearing. 'He accepts a family's hospitality, yet will neither drink nor eat, nor stand up to dance, nor sit down to play cards. I'm beginning to wonder if he might be an impostor.'

'He must have been invited because Mrs Davenant says he had a ticket,' Miss Wilton, the bejewelled shepherdess, replied, 'but she can't think of anyone who has not been accounted for.'

'Have you tried talking to him?' One of her companions asked.

'Oh, yes, but he must have disguised his voice, because I cannot place it at all, and I do know practically everyone who is anyone. And there is something very disconcerting about the way he stares at one.'

'Maybe we should lay wagers on the subject,' Kit suggested. 'Or a prize could be offered to the first person who guesses correctly.'

He was standing behind Isabel and

Sarah, but as he said this, he leaned forward and smiled at the former in rather an odd way. He waited, however, until they had sauntered back into the drawing-room before he asked her, 'I don't suppose you know who the black domino is?'

'I have not spoken to him,' she admitted, glancing across the room. The man in question had taken up his former position and their eyes met momentarily.

'Come along, then, before the dancing begins. Let's see what we can discover.' He exchanged looks with Sarah, who smothered a giggle.

Half-reluctantly, Isabel allowed herself to be trawled across the room. The black domino had chosen the most shady corner, his left shoulder leaning against the wall so half his mask lay in shadow. His other eye glittered in the reflected candlelight, but Isabel could not make out its colour.

'Come, come, old man, this won't do at all,' Kit greeted the austere figure with what seemed to Isabel to be inappropriate familiarity.

The domino did not reply, but she assumed he raised a questioning eyebrow.

'Skulking about in corners like this when there are half a dozen young ladies pining for want of a dancing partner.'

'I don't dance.'

The voice was low and though the words were abrupt, his manner was not. Isabel even thought she heard a note of regret in his voice.

'It's not difficult with the right partner,' Sarah assured him. 'You have been watching long enough to have noticed who the best dancers are.'

The black domino bowed and perhaps smiled. 'I should hate to inconvenience anyone with my blundering.'

Isabel shivered. Miss Wilton was right. It was disconcerting to be watched by that one eye while the other remained in shadow. It made her think of Edmund. Even the voice could be his. But that was absurd. Everyone knew there was no point in sending him an invitation.

'Did no-one ever tell you that only dancing masters dance without mistakes?' Kit replied. 'The sign of being a true gentleman is to dance badly.'

'Your dancing does credit to your parentage, sir.'

Isabel sensed the officer flush under his mask, unsure how to interpret the stranger's dry comment. Was he saying his dancing was too bad, or too good?

'I trust, sir, that you derive as much satisfaction from watching as other people have from dancing,' she intervened hastily.

The black domino turned towards her and she noticed that there was something unnatural about his left eye.

'A man cannot spend his entire life locked away with his books,' he said, in a voice that sent a shiver of recognition along Isabel's spine.

As he averted his face she realised what was wrong with his eye. It never blinked or moved because it was painted on to the mask so cleverly it was hardly possible to tell it wasn't real from a distance.

Isabel let the others babble on. She hardly even heard them. The unblinking eye, his voice, his figure. It was utterly impossible and yet she knew the black domino was Edmund Carwell.

Before she had time to recover, the musicians showed signs of resuming. Dazed, Isabel realised Kit had claimed her as his partner and he and Sarah were guiding her across the room.

'Well, is it or isn't it?' Sarah demanded as soon as they were out of earshot.

'What? Who?'

'Mr Carwell, of course.'

It was the 'of course' that came as a revelation to Isabel. This was their great secret — they had invited Edmund to the masquerade. They had introduced her to the black domino to see if she could identify him, so Kit could be sure of winning his bet.

Why had Edmund come? Should she go and talk to him, or would that arouse suspicion? The strength of her longing frightened her. He had made no attempt to approach her all night. And yet his words had been carefully chosen to let her know who he was. She could hardly prevent herself from glancing over her shoulder, to make sure he was still there.

'Well, there is nothing for it,' Captain Davenant said with a theatrical sigh. 'I'll have to set fire to his cloak, as if by accident, if that is the only way to unmask him.'

'Don't joke about such things,' Isabel cried out involuntarily. She felt sick to the pit of her stomach, remembering the terrible damage fire could inflict on a man's face.

'You're mighty serious all of a sudden,' Sarah remarked. 'Are you sure you don't know who he is? Or has the black domino cast his gloomy spell over you?'

'No, I don't know him,' Isabel replied

faintly, but she felt like a traitor. It was safer for Edmund that they didn't know. At least she hoped so. She couldn't be sure of anything just now.

While she was dancing, she was conscious of his eyes watching her. Whenever Kit or one of the others flirted with her, she wondered if he would misinterpret the signs and assume she had a favoured lover. In the end, she stole away to one of the windows for a breath of air, hoping he would join her. But Sarah was the first to locate her.

'There you are. What on earth are you doing?'

'I was just admiring the moonlight,' Isabel stammered. 'It seems a shame to be indoors on such a lovely night.'

She blushed, suddenly becoming conscious that Kit had come up behind Sarah.

'Perhaps we could walk about the garden by the light of the moon,' he suggested.

'Oh, yes,' Sarah squeezed his arm in delight.

Isabel protested about the impropriety, but both Kit and Sarah were determined now. Isabel had no choice. She couldn't let her friend go without a chaperone.

They stayed on the paths at Isabel's suggestion, because she was afraid the dew might stain the hem of her borrowed gown. Initially they kept their voices low, not wanting to attract attention, but gradually caution was cast aside. Voices became louder, jokes were tossed to and fro, laughter and even the odd shriek from Sarah echoed across the garden.

'Look at the reflection of the moon,' Sarah sighed, stepping on to the pier by the lake, to which a rowing boat had been moored, 'just like a magnificent pearl.'

'I'll dive in and fish it out for you, if you promise to be mine,' Kit murmured in a throaty whisper.

Isabel winced. If he could flirt so indiscriminately with either of them, why had she deluded herself he had any special interest in her?

'That's too high a price to pay,' Sarah retorted, smiling mischievously. She clasped her hands behind her back, dipped her head mock-demurely and said, 'I'd go and fish it out myself, if someone would take me out in the boat.'

'I'll do it in exchange for a kiss.'

'Done.'

'Sarah!' Isabel exclaimed in alarm.

'Ophelia, if you please, madam,' Sarah replied sweetly.

'There is nothing to worry about, I assure you, Miss Locke. I've been sculling myself since I was a small boy,' Kit intervened. 'Wait a moment while I fetch the oars from the boathouse.'

As soon as they were alone, Isabel turned to her friend. 'Let's go back to the house before he returns,' she said. 'It isn't safe, not at this hour of night.'

'Don't be so boring, Bel. I'd trust Captain Davenant with my life, wouldn't you?'

Isabel didn't reply, so Sarah carried

on wheedling. 'I can't back down now I have accepted his challenge. And anyway, I am Ophelia. I have an affinity with water.'

'And you know how Ophelia met her death.'

'Tush, tush, Miss Locke, are you trying to frighten my intrepid companion?' Kit's voice, so close behind her, made Isabel jump.

Sarah did not need much persuading. Isabel saw she had shaken her a little, but the chance of being in close proximity with Kit was too tempting. Sarah was so much in love that she would do anything to win his admiration.

In the blink of an eye, Kit and the oars were in the boat, rocking gently from side to side. He offered his hand to Sarah to help her down.

'Are you sure you won't join us?' He lowered his voice seductively and held out his hand to Isabel.

She realised his luminous gaze had no power over her any more. If she went, it would be solely as Sarah's chaperone. She glanced down. Her best shoes were already spoilt from walking across the damp ground. No, she could not risk damaging the borrowed gown.

'I'll stay here,' she said. 'There's hardly any room as it is.' She smiled in reply to Kit's curious glance.

She stayed on the pier, clinging to the railing, as the boat pushed off. Splashing oars, muted conversation, a muffled giggle. Isabel had never felt so alone in her life.

The air seemed colder now she was by herself. Involuntarily she found herself wishing Edmund Carwell were here. He would have understood how she felt about this beautiful but eerie night.

The ripples caused by the oars broke the reflection of the moon into a wavering line, like a white flame. Sarah laughed and dipped her fingers into the water, reaching for the nearest water lilies, but the stems were too tough for her to break. Their voices carried in the stillness.

'You wouldn't dare.'

'I would too.'

'Then prove it.'

'Very well, I will.'

And before Isabel could utter a cry of protest, Sarah had scrambled to her feet, rocking and swaying with the movement of the boat. She looked like a statue, her head lifted, the moon turning her gown silver.

Behind Isabel, there was a sudden rustle among the leaves. She glanced back over her shoulder, irrationally afraid for a moment. But she could make out nothing in the moonlight, which silvered the tips of the grass. Somewhere, far, far away, golden lights gleamed in the windows of the house. A bat flitted past.

Her eyes were only averted for half a minute, perhaps less, but it was long enough. Sarah's cry made her whip round. The boat was rocking, water slapping angrily against wood. Kit also cried out and half rose, stretching his arms towards Sarah. It happened so quickly, Isabel was not sure which of them was to blame, but a sudden movement made the boat pitch violently.

Arms flailed in the air, desperately trying to keep balance, but even before it happened, Isabel knew it was inevitable. The boat flipped over, tumbling out both its occupants. Sarah uttered a scream, which was choked off as she plunged into the water and vanished before Isabel's eyes.

9

For a second Isabel froze in horror, listening to the crashing of water, the muffled voices. A duck, disturbed from its sleep, protested loudly. Sarah's scream made Isabel's blood run cold.

'My leg — I'm trapped.'

Isabel knew exactly what had happened. The thick stems of the water lilies had got tangled round Sarah as she plunged into the water. If she could not fight her way free, she would be dragged under and drowned.

Every instinct urged her forward into the water to save her friend, despite the fact she could not swim. But common-sense told her she ought to seek help elsewhere. There was no other boat, no rope she could throw, no broken bough.

'Hold on, Sarah! I'm going to the house for help,' she called, backing away along the damp planks, unable to tear her eyes from the lake. She could make out the upturned boat and something indistinct — arms, heads — bobbing up and down on the shadowy surface.

It felt like an act of cowardice, to be running away from them. It might be all over long before she reached the house. Those could be Sarah's death cries. But still Isabel forced herself to turn and break into a run.

She had not taken more than ten steps, however, when she crashed against a black shape looming out of the darkness beneath the willows. Strong arms encircled her, steadying her balance. She looked up into a familiar face. Edmund Carwell had already ripped off his mask.

'Here, take this,' he breathed, disentangling himself from his cloak and thrusting it into her arms. He ripped open the buttons of his coat and waistcoat and wrenched off his shoes without stopping to undo the buckles.

'Keep her head above water — I'm

coming,' he called as he launched himself into the blackness.

'Edmund, be careful.'

The words escaped her before she could stop herself. Isabel hesitated, her heart lurching painfully. Her arms were full of clothes, still warm from his body. Should she run to the house?

It was a meaningless question. She had no power to go, not when two of the people she cared for most in the world were in danger.

The two men were calling to each other above the splashing of water, but the position of the upturned boat made it impossible for Isabel to see what was happening. And Sarah. What about Sarah? She could not hear her voice any more.

Someone was swimming towards shore. Dear God, let them all be safe. Isabel draped Edmund's coat and waistcoat over the railing and shook out the black cloak, ready for whoever needed it most.

'Leave the boat,' Edmund called.

'You can fetch it tomorrow.'

His voice was closer than she had expected and her heart leapt with relief. He was coming first and the white, nebulous figure he was towing with him must be Sarah. Kit took his advice and laboured after him, his movements slower because he had been in the water longer and was weighed down by his costume.

Isabel hurried to the end of the pier to meet them. Edmund had reached shallow water so he could stand upright and gather Sarah up in his arms. Her head slumped against his shoulder, but she gave a weak, rasping cough.

She's alive, Isabel thought. Thank God, she's alive. Clinging to the railing with one hand, she reached out with the other to pull Edmund up on to the pier. Kit was not far behind, beginning to wade through the water.

They looked exhausted from the ordeal, hardly able to speak through their wheezing and coughing. Edmund laid Sarah down on the cloak Isabel had spread on the dew-drenched grass. While he pumped water out of her lungs, Isabel tugged Kit on to the shore. He had kicked off his boots, she noticed, to make himself lighter.

'Take my coat, Davenant,' Edmund panted, wrapping Sarah in the cloak before lifting her up in his arms again. Kit protested, but ignoring him, the other man turned towards Isabel. 'Run ahead to the house and warn them we're coming.'

The moon emerged, tracing a line down his profile from forehead to jaw. His chest was still heaving beneath the sodden white shirt, his dark hair plastered to his forehead.

She was exhausted long before she reached the house, but she forced herself on, across endless lawns, up shallow stone steps, past statues and fountains, aiming solely for the golden lights of the windows. She knew the worst was over and compelled herself not to think about what might have happened if Edmund had not been there.

Her appearance in the ballroom caused a sensation. She was so breathless, she could barely speak, her curls dishevelled, her gown splashed.

'Accident — by the lake,' she wheezed, her stays crushing her lungs. 'The Captain — Miss Waite — Mr Carwell — all safe. They're — they're coming — right behind me . . . '

Some had already dashed out to see what was happening before she had finished speaking. Someone pushed her into a chair and wafted a bottle of hartshorn beneath her nose.

She lifted her head at Mrs Waite's cry of dismay. Edmund had just entered. With her hair and her gown bedraggled and her remaining wreaths trailing, Sarah looked as limp and dead as the real Ophelia.

Trapped behind a wall of ice, Isabel watched the other masqueraders flit past. Sarah's appearance caused such a reaction, Isabel wondered how many of them even noticed the man who carried her. Tall, with his shirt clinging to his chest and arms, his eye-patch removed or lost at some point so that his damaged eye and scarred cheek were visible. Somewhere between the shifting, bobbing heads, she also caught a glimpse of Kit Davenant before all three were bundled up in blankets and hustled away.

And so it fell to Isabel to try to explain what had happened. She told the story over and over, answering dozens of questions. A glass was forced into her hand from which she took fiery sips. Again and again she heard expressions of wonder about Edmund Carwell's presence. Had he been invited? How had he chanced to be nearby at the critical moment?

And then other, muted comments became audible, remarks on his appearance and speculation about whether or not he was blind in one eye.

The shock began to sink in. Isabel found she was shaking uncontrollably, her teeth chattering in spite of the warmth. Most of all, she wanted to hide somewhere and cry. But that was impossible.

In the end her father intervened. 'That's enough for one night. Come along, Bel, the carriage is waiting.'

Isabel rose and he put his arm around her to guide her to the door. She glanced round, hoping for one more glimpse of Edmund. Footsteps on the staircase made them look up. Mr Waite hurried down a few more steps.

'Have you seen Carwell? I wanted to thank him properly.'

'I'm sure he cannot be far away,' Mr Locke said. 'How is Sarah?'

'Oh, she'll do well enough. Swallowed some water and dented her pride. Mrs Davenant has offered to put us all up for the night.'

Vaguely Isabel heard a carriage thundering away. The evening had come to an abrupt end for the entire party.

'I'd best get Isabel home before the

vultures tear her to pieces,' Mr Locke said. 'Give our regards to Mrs Waite and Sarah.'

Being away from the clacking voices was a relief. But the carriage rocked violently over the badly repaired road, reminding her of the pitching boat. She could not allow herself to cry just yet, because she knew she would not be able to stop.

⋆   ⋆   ⋆

Isabel passed a long, broken night. Whenever she shut her eyes, she saw the accident again, playing over and over, as if something had become trapped in her mind. She cried sporadically, but tears brought no relief and her eyes were red and sore when she woke at dawn.

Her father agreed it was necessary to call at Davenant Hall after a late but brief breakfast. Kit had gathered quite a circle of admirers around him, all very anxious about his health and full of admiration for his courage. Isabel noticed that a Miss Wilton was there among the crowd, her eyes solicitous, her voice cooing like a dove's.

Mrs Waite was still there. Her daughter had been given strict instructions to stay in bed until the doctor called as she had shown signs of an incipient cold from being immersed in the icy, spring-fed lake.

'Not that I expect her to obey me,' Mrs Waite added feelingly. 'She probably got up as soon as the door shut behind me.'

'What about Mr Carwell? How is he?' Isabel asked, glancing around. She would not feel at ease till she had seen him again.

'Nobody knows. It seems he stole away last night amid the confusion. Mr Davenant and my husband have gone to Longwood to make enquiries.'

Mrs Waite leaned forward and dropped her voice confidentially. 'It's odd the way the human mind works, isn't it? Mr Carwell brushed off all my attempts to thank him for saving our poor child, and seemed more anxious to retrieve his waistcoat than anything else.'

Isabel tried to smile. Could the missing waistcoat be the one she had made for him? She had been so convinced Edmund would be here that his absence felt like a bereavement. But she understood why he wanted to avoid public notice.

Mrs Waite was already talking about inviting him to dine with them and Isabel guessed she would not be the only one. She ought to be glad that circumstances had forced him into making new acquaintances. She would be able to see him more often, as long as he did not reject their offers.

She was allowed to go up to Sarah's room. As she tapped at the door, she could hear running steps and the frantic rustling of sheets before Sarah called out, 'Come in.' No doubt Mrs Waite had been right and Sarah had got out of bed without permission.

She smiled at the sight of Isabel, but her eyes were full of tears.

'Sarah, what on earth is the matter?'

'I was hoping you would come,' she said, choking off a sob. 'You were right about Kit. I should have listened to you.'

'What has he done to you? Last night . . . ' Isabel began, but Sarah cut her short.

'I don't mean that. I — I heard something this morning.'

Isabel felt a chill steal over her, prickling her arms beneath her elbow length sleeves. Sarah dashed the back of her hand across her eyes.

'I happened to be by the window because I needed a breath of air and I'm not at all ill, no matter what Mamma says, and they were right beneath my window, so their voices drifted up to me.'

'Who?'

'Captain Davenant and Miss Wilton. I didn't hear what she said, only she sounded angry or upset. And then he said, 'I was under the impression my advances were not welcome and I did not wish to plague you', or something like that.'

'Oh, Sarah,' Isabel murmured, hugging her friend. This piece of news only confirmed what she already suspected about Kit.

'Miss Wilton didn't seem to know how to reply, so he added in a low tone, 'If I thought I had any hope of being accepted, I would go and speak to your father at once'.'

Sarah's voice trembled and trailed away. Isabel could see she was upset, but she hoped she would recover from her infatuation in time.

'I'm so sorry, Bel,' Sarah said. 'I thought you had stolen him from me and I hated you sometimes, but now it seems he was toying with us both.'

'Don't worry about me,' Isabel assured her, squeezing her tightly. Tears brimmed over in Sarah's big blue eyes.

She managed to cheer Sarah by abusing Kit roundly and then making plans for what they would do when Sarah was allowed to come home and resume her ordinary life.

Mr Davenant and Mr Waite had not returned by the time Isabel left, so it was not till the following morning that she heard the news. Edmund Carwell had received them, not without reluctance, but he had accepted invitations to dine both at Davenant Hall and the parsonage over the next two days. Isabel knew she was not important enough to be invited to the hall, but she was almost bound to be one of the party at the parsonage.

Sure enough, a note arrived from Mrs Waite during the course of the day and Isabel accepted with alacrity, knowing her father had no other engagement on the next day. She took special care of her appearance, but when they entered the parlour, Mrs Waite greeted them with a woebegone face.

'Oh dear, I'm dreadfully afraid the Davenants have frightened away our

161

guest,' she said, waving a note towards them. 'I did wonder if it was wise to invite such a large party to meet Mr Carwell, but Mrs Davenant was so keen to show off her new acquisition as she called him. Now he has written to say he is unwell and cannot come.'

Something more than disappointment welled up inside Isabel. Could it be just an excuse? He must have known she would be there. Perhaps he was avoiding her. But when she sat down beside her hostess, she got a closer look at the letter. It hardly looked like Edmund's handwriting at all, it was so untidy and straggling. Could he have asked someone else to write it? Or maybe he really was ill.

The thought haunted her throughout the evening and the night that followed. Kit Davenant intercepted her and Sarah while they were out for their morning walk and ignored their coolness towards him.

'How was the dinner for the conquering hero last night?' he asked.

Sarah grudgingly admitted Mr Carwell had not been able to come.

'An odd fellow,' he remarked. 'You didn't miss much in the way of conversation — he spent most of the evening shivering and coughing and answering questions as if he hadn't heard them properly.'

'But that's not like him at all. He must have been ill.'

Kit merely shrugged. 'I can only tell you what I saw.'

Isabel couldn't bear to think of Edmund alone in his abandoned mansion, maybe patiently waiting for death, not even trying to fight off the fever that had seized him. She could not bear to let him go without a struggle.

She hurried home only to find her father was out on business. There was no saying how late it might be before he returned. She could not stand the uncertainty a moment longer. She knew it was improper, but she had enough money saved out of her quarterly allowance to hire a chaise. She sent out Eliza directly to fetch a carriage and scribbled a hasty note to her father.

She was ready to go by the time the chaise appeared at the door. With every second her mission seemed more important. Suppose she was already too late.

'Where to?' the coachman asked as she set her foot on the bottom step.

'Longwood Priory.'

10

The journey seemed agonisingly slow to Isabel. There was a delay at the gates and it was only because she gave her name that they were allowed to enter.

The drive felt longer than ever, twisting and turning through the leafy tunnel. Isabel gripped the edge of the window, barely able to sit still a moment longer as she craned her head towards the house.

In her haste to get up, she caught the hem of her petticoat on her heel and was forced to waste precious seconds untangling it, if she did not want to topple headfirst out of the carriage.

The door of the house opened as she set her foot on the gravel. Her head shot up, but it was only Mrs Beecroft.

'Oh, Miss Locke, this is a surprise,' the housekeeper panted as she trundled down the steps. She was obviously in a flurry, her eyes round and frightened, and a strand of hair coming loose from under her widow's cap. 'Is your father not with you?'

'No, he was not at home when I set out. But I couldn't bear to stay there and not know the truth. Is Mr Carwell very ill?'

She should have sent a messenger. She could see that now. She could not imagine the housekeeper allowing her to see Edmund, no matter how ill he was. She had been a fool to come.

'The doctor says if the fever doesn't break soon, he can't vouch for his recovery.'

Isabel's knees buckled beneath her at this hoarse whisper and she was forced to grip the balustrade for support. Mrs Beecroft exclaimed in alarm, seeing how pale she had grown.

'How long has he been this bad?' Isabel faltered.

'He's not been well since he returned from the masquerade, only he wouldn't admit it or let me send for the doctor. I didn't even find out what had happened till the gentlemen called. And yesterday, he was so determined to go to the parsonage, though his valet says he could scarcely stand upright while he was dressing for dinner. He wouldn't listen to reason, no matter what I said, but just as he reached the carriage, his legs gave way. Even then, he insisted on writing the note of apology himself before he let us assist him up to bed.'

Isabel shuddered. She thought she understood. He had been as desperate to see her, as she was to see him and nothing, not even physical weakness, was allowed to stand in his way. They had reached the great hall by now. Mrs Beecroft had obviously pent up her anxiety for so long, she found it impossible to stop talking.

'I can't think why they let him come home like that, soaked to the skin and nothing but a blanket to keep him warm. I begged him to go to bed and he said he would, but I heard him pacing about the house for hours afterwards.'

In justice to the Davenants, Isabel felt obliged to tell her that they had offered Edmund a bed for the night, but the housekeeper hardly seemed to hear her.

'I'm so dreadfully afraid as he has undermined his constitution these past few weeks. He's thrown himself into making improvements to the home farm and the tenants' cottages. I thought it was a good thing at first, but he's been out in all kinds of weather.'

All that work, just to take his mind off his loneliness.

'You must let me see him,' Isabel whispered, unable to raise her voice.

'Oh, Miss Locke, I'm not sure that's wise.'

'Please, if he is going to die, I must see him again.' I must make my peace with him, she added silently in her head.

Mrs Beecroft hesitated, then unwillingly she led the way along the gallery and up the spiral staircase. There were two doors at the top of the stairs, one leading to Edmund's study, the other to a tiny dressing room, in which a bed had been made, so a servant could sleep within calling distance of the third, inner chamber.

It came back to Isabel that Mrs Beecroft has told her once that these were the rooms Edmund had stayed in as a child, out of the way of the adults, and that therefore he had chosen this suite as his own when he became master of the house, despite the fact they were much smaller than the main bedrooms at the back of the house.

Mrs Beecroft entered first. There was a soft rustle as a maid rose from her seat by the bed. Mrs Beecroft dismissed her with the wave of her hand. The curtains had been drawn around the bed, but the housekeeper parted them gently.

'There's a visitor for you, sir.'

In a house where visitors were scarce, the world seemed to hang in the air like the tolling of a bell. Isabel was shocked by his appearance. Edmund's face had grown gaunt, his cheeks hollow and his eyes black caverns beneath the high ridge of his forehead. He was pale, save for a feverish flush, and his lips were cracked and parched.

Mrs Beecroft had taken care not to approach him on his blind side, but he turned his head towards them, pain in his eye, the parody of a polite, welcoming smile on his lips. It froze there as he gazed at Isabel.

'Delirium,' he whispered to himself, trying to reassure himself that all was well, that he had not completely lost his mind.

'No, sir, I'm not a figment of your imagination,' Isabel replied.

Hardly conscious that Mrs Beecroft was still in the room, though she had withdrawn a few steps from the bed, Isabel laid her hand against his scarred cheek. Her fingers were icy from the journey. His skin was so hot, she almost pulled away as if she had touched live coals.

'How are you?' she asked gently.

'Better for seeing you.'

The sheets rustled. He freed his hand in order to take hold of her wrist and moved her hand across his throbbing forehead. He closed his eyes to savour the moment.

'Mrs Beecroft,' Isabel said, peering round her shoulder, 'we need an ice cold compress.'

'This is better,' Edmund murmured.

'My hands will soon be warm. The compress will soothe you for longer.'

A deep sigh burst from his chest and he squeezed his eyes tighter. He swallowed painfully and brought on a fit of coughing.

There was a half-full glass on the table beside the bed and between the two of them, the women managed to raise him to a sitting position. While the housekeeper plumped his pillows, he leaned against Isabel and took cautious sips from the glass she held to his lips.

He slumped back against the pillows,

exhausted. Isabel placed the compress on his forehead before motioning to the housekeeper to go.

'I'll sit with him for a while,' she said, 'Oh, and will you dismiss my chaise? I have the money here.'

She had intended only a quick visit, but now she knew no power on earth could persuade her to leave until the crisis was over, one way or the other. Keeping the carriage waiting indefinitely would be an expensive mistake.

Mrs Beecroft looked doubtful, but she did as she was bid. Isabel seated herself on the bed and placed her hand on his scarred cheek, knowing what the gesture meant to him. She could not think of any other way in which to show him how she felt. A shiver trickled down him at her touch, but otherwise he lay so still, she wondered if he had fallen asleep.

There were so many things she wanted to say to him, but he was in no fit state to listen. She did not even care about the impropriety of being alone in the bedroom of a man to whom she was neither married, engaged nor related.

She shifted to make herself more comfortable and his right eye sprang open.

'Don't go.'

'I won't. I promise.'

But his eye remained fixed on her and she could see that, slowly and laboriously, he was trying to reason something out, in spite of his fever.

'You called me Edmund,' he said.

'What?'

'Just as I jumped into the lake.'

The flush crept along Isabel's cheek. She had forgotten that slip of the tongue. She didn't know what to say.

'Why did you come?'

'I wanted to see you.'

Another thought struck him and he lifted from the pillows as if to search the room. 'Your father . . . '

'I came alone.'

That made him gaze long and hard at her, his mind moving as sluggishly as a waterwheel in a drought. Isabel could not bear the intensity of his gaze for long and dropped her eyes to the collar of his white nightshirt, which was visible above the sheet. She saw his throat convulse as he swallowed.

'You shouldn't be here. What will people say?'

'They can say what they like.'

But Edmund shook his head, dislodging his nightcap and the compress. 'Your reputation . . . '

'It doesn't matter.' She silenced him by laying her hand on his dry lips.

She watched the light change in his fever-bright eye and as she was about to slide her fingers away, she felt his lips move to kiss them. To bridge the awkward moment, she tugged his cap into place, moistened and wrung out the compress and replaced it on his brow.

'You ought to sleep,' she said. 'It's the only way you will get well again.'

'I'd rather die in your arms than live here without you.'

His words struck her heart like a dagger.

'You mustn't say such things, you mustn't think that way.' She tried to laugh, but it came out as a sob. 'You promised to take me skating.'

'I don't want your pity, Isabel.'

'I'm not offering you pity.'

Edmund closed his eye again and she felt a twinge of guilt. He looked so ill, far too ill to be discussing such things.

'I'm offering you love,' she whispered, afraid he would hear her, and afraid he would not.

He did not reply, but the room was so breathlessly still, she heard his lashes brush against his pillowcase. He was shivering, despite being so hot to touch.

'Stay with me till I fall asleep,' he murmured, 'and then go home.'

She promised to do the first and only silently withheld her consent to his second request. Gradually he slid into an uneasy sleep, but Isabel didn't move. He mustn't, mustn't die. He had over-exerted himself and it was all her fault. She could feel the heat emanating from his body even when she wasn't touching him.

In the end, worried because nobody had rang the bell, Mrs Beecroft ventured back to the room and found Isabel still perched sideways on the bed. She managed to coax her out of the room, promising her a bite to eat. Isabel was surprised by how dark it had grown. She was stiff from sitting motionless for so long.

There was a fire in the prior's parlour downstairs, but obviously it had been recently lit, since the air hit her like a block of ice. To be honest, Isabel had no appetite, but she forced herself to eat so as not to offend the housekeeper. She was still picking at a slice of cold meat when the doctor arrived. She wondered if Mrs Beecroft had been expecting him and had deliberately lured her out of the sickroom.

She seemed to wait for hours until she heard their steps enter the great hall on their way down. She stole across to the door to listen.

'There's nothing more I can do. It's

in God's hands now.'

Rousing herself, she hurried back to the sickroom. The change in Edmund's condition petrified her. He had begun muttering in his delirium, rattling off staccato phrases too fast for her to be able to decipher them.

She was still at his bedside when her father arrived. He had set out as soon as he received Isabel's note, despite Eliza's protests that he hadn't eaten.

Edmund had not improved. Several times he had thrown off his blankets to cool himself, only to be seized immediate by shivering fits. Once he had sat bolt upright, his eye half-open but blank, and he grappled with Isabel when she prevented him from getting out of bed. He had even called her name, but failed to recognise her when she responded.

She turned towards the door at the sound of steps. Tears glittered below the surface of her eyes.

'Papa,' she said, 'I don't want him to die.'

★ ★ ★

It was not until the early hours of the following morning that the fever broke and Edmund sank into a profound and death-like sleep. Isabel had stayed by his side all that time, despite being urged to go and rest.

She knew she was exhausted because the room swam around her when she finally lay down in the bed that had been prepared for her. But strangely enough her tiredness kept her awake, reminding her that her head ached and her limbs were weary, whenever she was in any danger of forgetting it.

Her thoughts churned round and round, picturing Edmund's sufferings, remembering his jump into the lake at Davenant Hall, throwing up snatches of conversation, hinting at how black the world would be without him now that she knew she loved him. And guilt — guilt about all the things she had said and done and shouldn't have, or all the things that had been left unsaid and undone.

Eventually she slept, then woke, terrified that Edmund had relapsed and nobody had told her. She knew she ought to get up and yet, in the middle of those ghastly thoughts, she fell asleep again, only to be tormented by nightmares.

When she woke again, guilt made her drag herself to a seated position at once, despite the smarting of her eyes. She stretched out her hand for the bell and then realised she could not bear to hear the news from a servant if Edmund had died during the night.

She had slept in her shift. The rest of her clothes were draped over the back of a chair, where she had left them the previous night. Getting dressed was a frustrating process. Her arms ached long before she was finished and scalding tears rushed into her eyes more than once.

Her fingers fumbled when she tried to tie knots and fasten hooks. Luckily her stays had lace at the front and back, so she could manage them by herself, but she got lost among the billowing folds of her petticoats when she lifted them over her head. Getting her arm into the first sleeve of her gown was easy — finding the other nearly impossible. And all the while, time was dripping away.

She was forced to pause outside her door to take her bearings. The house seemed both frighteningly familiar and unfamiliar. She could not even remember coming this way to bed the previous night. Nothing but deathly silence all around her. Her footsteps on the spiral staircase seemed deafeningly loud, though she tried to tread softly. The door creaked as she pushed it open.

'He's still fast asleep,' Mrs Beecroft whispered, 'and by the look of you, you should be too.'

Once she was satisfied the house-keeper had told her the truth — Edmund's breathing was so slow and imperceptible, she could hardly believe he was alive at first — Isabel accepted the most comfortable chair in the room and let herself drowse away the hours, while keeping one ear open for any sound from the bed.

★ ★ ★

It was late afternoon by the time he woke, weak but lucid. The first thing he saw as he opened his eye was Isabel's face stooped over him.

'I thought I'd dreamt you,' he said.

'No, I'm really here.'

'How long have I been asleep?'

'You were delirious for the entire night and have slept away the best part of a day.'

'And you have been here all this time?'

'Most of it.' She blushed and looked away, glad he had no memory of how she had cried during the night and begged him not to die when he was at the height of his fever.

'That conversation we had — I didn't dream that either, did I?'

181

She shook her head. How much did he remember?

'You should go, while there is time to salvage your reputation.'

'You think there is still a hope for that?' Isabel asked, with a pale smile. 'How long must I stay here until I force you to play the honourable part and marry me?'

Edmund winced. 'Don't joke about such things. I can't bear it.'

'I'm not joking,' she said, but something crumbled deep inside her. He wasn't going to propose. She had overstepped the bounds of propriety to no good purpose. She averted her face and blinked back the tears of exhaustion and despair. There was a long pause. He sighed.

'No, I've no right to take advantage of your vulnerability. You are grateful to me for helping to save your friend, that's all. You would regret it in time if you were saddled with a deformed and embittered husband.'

Her eyes flashed at his face. 'You're

the handsomest, kindest man I know. This has nothing to do with Sarah. I loved you a long time before then, only I didn't realise it.' She dropped her head again, knowing she had said too much.

'Isabel.' The urgency of his tone made her look up. 'Do you really mean it? You will marry me?'

Isabel nodded, her throat suddenly too full for speech, and laid her hand against his withered cheek. The light dawned slowly in his eye, a smile began to tug at his lips.

'Kiss me,' he said, making an effort to sit up.

But not for long. Isabel pressed his shoulders back down on the bed and lowered her face towards his. He freed his arm from the covers and curled his fingers round the nape of her neck, burying them in her hair as he drew her face closer and closer until their lips touched.

We do hope that you have enjoyed reading this large print book.

Did you know that all of our titles are available for purchase?

We publish a wide range of high quality large print books including:
Romances, Mysteries, Classics
General Fiction
Non Fiction and Westerns

Special interest titles available in large print are:
The Little Oxford Dictionary
Music Book, Song Book
Hymn Book, Service Book

Also available from us courtesy of Oxford University Press:
Young Readers' Dictionary
(large print edition)
Young Readers' Thesaurus
(large print edition)

For further information or a free brochure, please contact us at:
Ulverscroft Large Print Books Ltd.,
The Green, Bradgate Road, Anstey,
Leicester, LE7 7FU, England.
Tel: (00 44) **0116 236 4325**
Fax: (00 44) **0116 234 0205**

BELLE OF THE BALL

Anne Holman

When merchandise is stolen from the shop where Isabel Hindley works, she and the other shop assistants are under suspicion. So when Lady Yettington is observed going out of the shop without paying for goods, Isabel accuses her ladyship of theft, making her nephew, Charles Yettington, furious. But things are more complicated when Lady Yettington is put under surveillance, and more merchandise goes missing. Isabel and Charles plan to find out who is responsible.

THE KINDLY LIGHT

Valerie Holmes

Annie Darton's life was happiness itself, living with her father, the lighthouse keeper of Gannet Rock, until an accident changed their lives forever. Forced to move, Annie's path crosses with the attractive stranger, Zachariah Rudd. Shrouded in mystery, undoubtedly hiding something, he becomes steadily more involved in Annie's life, especially when the new lighthouse keeper is murdered. Annie finds herself drawn into the mysteries around her. Only by resolving the past can she look to the future, whatever the cost!